Enjoy the
book!

~ R.A. Dillow

FIGHTING CHANGE

WEREWITCH BOOK 1

By,

R.A. Dillow

Slaughter. A bite that won't fade. An unknown evil that just won't quit. Who do you trust when you're not sure if you can trust yourself?

Chapter 1

Welcome to Werewolf Country

LEE

I breathe in deeply of the early morning mountain air as I stand in the backyard. It's cool this morning, but warm enough where I don't need a jacket, my thin cotton shirt is just enough. I smell the horses at the far end of the pasture, the cattle up on the rise, the squirrels in the trees and the rabbits on the ground. I breathe it all in and a rush of adrenaline goes through me. I look down at my hands and see the nails have started to grow and change and my mouth turns into a grim line.

I look back out to the horizon, curling my fingers into tight fists. The sharp nails dig into my palm, but I'm careful not to spill blood. I breathe in deeply again and I know my brown eyes have shifted to that eerie blue and I know, I know I've pushed it as far as I can. I don't intend to turn today, or tomorrow, or the next day or the next, so it's time to stop tempting the beast inside and get on with morning chores. I shake my head and my human side feels more in control as I head down to the barns before breakfast.

My name is Lee, well if I'm being honest my real name is Paisley, but no one calls me that – ever, not friends and no longer family. And I do mean ever. My name is Lee, period. Got it? Ok. Anyway, my full name is Lee Rose Montgomery and I am a werewolf. Yeah, that's right I'm one of those hairy beasts, well with a few exceptions anyway.

I refuse to change; that's right, I refuse to let the wolf out, which is a really really bad thing. I am a werewolf who refuses to change into a werewolf…yeah it's not a good situation.

I have remained in human form for the last 3 months, even though I've been told I shouldn't. The pack that took me in used to tell me I can't stay in human form, but that stopped when they saw me remain a human through the first Full Moon. Oh it wasn't easy…there was lots of screaming and agony, so much agony. An uncontrollable shiver goes through me at the memory of the pain. I felt like I was killing myself by not changing, and maybe bit by bit I am.

I am part of the Centennial Mountain Werewolf Pack and we live up in the high valleys, along the snow-capped mountains of western Montana. Specifically we live on the eastern side of the Centennial Mountain range.

These mountains are beautiful, the trees so tall, the air so fresh…maybe it's all due to these heightened werewolf senses or maybe it is just that beautiful here.

There's a sense of wildness here unlike any I have every experienced anywhere else, and that wildness calls to a part of my soul...like a siren's song.

I'm not originally from this part of the country, so the beautiful scenery practically overwhelms me even now when I've been here for the whole summer. I've done a lot of changing this summer, from what I am to where I live to how I dress. I dress more like a country ranch hand these days in the typical boots, blue jeans, and t-shirts. Yeah I still wear some makeup, but since I have the job of a ranch hand and a farmer's tan going on...I just don't get real girly anymore. What's the point?

I'm not sure where I was born, but I was raised in the small town of Yellow Springs in southwest Ohio by two loving parents, Charles and Beth Montgomery. They weren't my birth parents, but they sure loved me as if they really had been my real parents. I don't know who my real parents are, and I don't care. They didn't want anything to do with me, and I don't want anything to do with them.

Yellow Springs has a population just under 3,800. In a town that size everybody knows everybody. Although to be fair this is what I thought of as a small town until I came out west – these little western towns bring a whole new meaning to the words: small town living. I enjoyed growing up where I did though without the major cities and high crime rates. Life in Yellow Springs was like living in a different time, a simpler time. That may sound a little cheesy, but it's true.

I was just a small town girl with small town dreams. I spent my whole life in Yellow Springs and so did my best friend Jeannie. She and I only lived a few houses apart and then after graduating high school we both attended the local college; Jeannie because her family couldn't afford to send her to a major university far away, and me because it allowed me to stay close to home and help my aging parents. It absolutely devastated me when they passed away. They were killed by a drunk driver two years ago. It happened just after the New Year and was the worst time in my life. Jeannie was the one to help get me through it; she helped me put their affairs in order, organize their property, and she convinced me not to quit school. Jeannie is the best friend I've ever had.

My friend Jeannie and I decided to go on a cross-country road trip after graduating college – we thought it would be fun to take some time away before we got serious with jobs and such. It was a last opportunity to have fun and just be "kids." I didn't realize when we loaded up the truck and left Ohio this past May that it would be the last trip Jeannie would ever take. It was supposed to be fun and simple. I remember small details of the trip as we meandered our way through the Midwest and made it to Glacier National Park a week before the Memorial Day weekend rush.

I pause in shoveling out the horse stalls as I think of Jeannie. I stare at the wall and try to remember all the good things, but I can feel myself getting lost into the horror of that last memory.

I remember how quiet and peaceful it was…how great we thought it was to be out in the middle of nowhere right up close to nature. After years of busy classes and then going through my parents' deaths, it was just great getting out of Ohio. I remember smelling the fresh air that morning and thinking life couldn't get better than this – I was so stupid.

Jeannie and I had setup camp, just a basic 4-man tent around a fire pit in the woods near some hiking trails. We were surrounded by tall pine trees and that evergreen smell filtering through the air made me think of Christmas. Silly? Perhaps, but pine trees have always made me think of Christmas.

I remember it was warm that day, but there was still a chill in the air when the wind blew; we were in northern Montana after all. We decided to go for an afternoon hike – I don't remember what trail we took, I think my brain has blocked that part out. One moment we were laughing and the next Jeannie was screaming.

After a great morning hike and an afternoon spent at one of the lakes we headed back to camp. By the placement of the sun it was moving into the late evening hours and we still had a good 3 miles before reaching our campsite. It had been a great day and we had taken some awesome photos. I remember the sparkle in her green eyes as she talked about her boyfriend Mike and how the wind was whipping her blonde hair across her face. She turned left to head down the last trail that would take us back to our truck and tent, when suddenly a furry blur came out of the trees to our right. It slammed into Jeannie with so much force it carried both of them into the trees on our left. I remember my brain thinking it was a wolf and I quickly grabbed a branch to club the beast with. I smacked it on the back of the head a few times, but it wasn't letting Jeannie go.

I begin to gulp for air as I remember the look in her eyes, the sheer terror as the beast clamped down on her throat, shutting her off mid-scream as the animal's teeth ripped her throat out. I remember the gurgling sounds as her blood rushed out and the light of life left her eyes.

It all happened so fast and still I smacked the beast, hoping I could save her even though I knew it was hopeless. Moving quickly, so fast my eyes could barely follow the beast turned on me. I say beast, I say wolf, but it seemed like a mixture of both. It had eerily bright blue eyes – not the shade of blue mine turn into when the wolf is present, they were more phosphorescent that's what I remember as it launched its body at me, throwing me off balance and I hit the ground hard.

I tried to keep fighting as I felt the heat from its breath and then it clamped its jaws onto my elbow and I let out a cry of pain. I felt the bones crunch and then it swung me through the air and my head hit something hard. Whatever I hit must have knocked me out because the next thing I remember is waking up to the sound of panicked voices. Someone was shouting to call an

ambulance, a person leaned over me to tell me I was
going to be ok, but I knew they were lying because my
best friend was dead and nothing was going to bring her
back. I didn't realize then how not ok I was going to be.

~~~~~~

I woke up in a hospital the next morning with a
violent headache and memories of a horror I wish I
could forget. The doctors told me I was in deep shock
over the attack because the beast I was describing was
bigger than any wolf that had been seen in the area. I
didn't say much to anybody after that because I wasn't
crazy. The beep beep of the heart monitor was all that
kept me company while my mind played the events of
the past day before over and over again. Jeannie's dying
became a loop in my head playing over and over again
and the few times I drifted into a restless sleep I found
something viciously snarling in the dark waiting to
finish me off.

The police came to get my statement and some Park Rangers were there as well. I asked what would happen to Jeannie, and I can remember the sympathy in their eyes as they explained she was at the County Coroner's office awaiting a family member to identify her body and be there for the transfer back to Ohio.

Her body they said, her body…and the thought alone made me want to vomit. Her body wasn't supposed to be lying in a cold drawer in a sterilized room. She was supposed to be laughing and taking pictures as we explored the beauties of Glacier Park. The rest of the day passed in a fog as the nurses did their periodic checks and Jeannie's parents called to ask me what happened. I balled like a child as I could barely get the story out. I apologized a thousand times, but they didn't blame me…they should have blamed me!

Two days later I woke up to see Martha and Gregory in my hospital room. That was the first time I met the Alpha and his mate. They said they were going to look after me now because I would never be the same.

I can still feel the tingle from where I was bitten. My left elbow has healed up just fine, except for the teeth marks, they are still there. Pale white scratches that no amount of superhuman healing could erase from my skin. Part of me is tempted to just rip the flesh from my body to get rid of it. Sure it would hurt, but I mean the flesh would grow back, so what was I waiting for? I should just rip it out I think again as I move all the straw and manure to the giant dumpster behind the barns , but I couldn't. No matter how much I hated the memory of that night and how it still haunted my nightmares – it was the strongest reminder I had of what happened.

Jeannie and the werewolf who attacked us were mixed in with that bite and I just couldn't erase it like it never occurred. I feel the tremors roll through me and the queasiness enters my stomach, oh crap I think I might be sick. I shake my head, trying to forget the memory. Oh Jeannie.

I've got to stop thinking about that night because if I don't I'm going to lose it and I don't need that right now.

Life has been a definite change of pace with the Centennial pack. Oh I'm technically on the bottom of the pile when it comes to pack rank, but we're all aware I'm not submissive, which in itself puts me above several of the purebloods in the pack. Mmm, seems like I was destined to cause problems here. I won't change, I am not the rank in the pack that a non-pureblood like me should be, and I refuse to even talk about the idea of finding a mate. Three for three, yay me.

Anyway, since I refuse to change the pack that has taken me in has pretty much put all the wolves on babysitter mode. Oh, and I get to look forward to all those lovely lectures about how I should change otherwise I'm going to snap and if I snap I may just kill someone.

I know I may still be fairly new to this whole "werewolf" thing, but I KNOW that it's really really bad what I am doing, but I can't change, not when she is watching me – and I feel her always, always watching me.

I want to change, I want to shift and feel the wolf take over. I want to feel the rush I see the others get to feel. I want to lope through the woods and chase the rabbits and squirrels; I want to lap at the water in my wolf form. Every time the breeze kicks up I want to give in and become a wolf. I want to go for a run in the moonlight and chase down a deer in the woods, but I just can't and its killing me a little every day, that's how much power she has over me.

Martha, the alpha female of my new pack keeps wanting to discuss my refusal to change, and out of the politeness and mandatory respect I must give to the alphas, I listen, but I don't divulge much. I don't just give her the mandatory respect anymore though; I give her real respect because she is a good person, if werewolves are still considered to be people, I think with a chuckle as I continue on with my morning chores.

Martha has been giving me daily werewolf classes, what I sarcastically like to call "Werewolf 101" as it literally is teaching me the basics of our history, yes our history as I am a werewolf now. She has been teaching me where the bloodlines originated from and how wolves have done their best to stay out of the limelight.

It does seem a little shady how werewolves came to be...as if the wolves aren't that sure just how werewolves came to be.

Was it God?

Magic?

A punishment from Satan?

Nobody seems to know the answer to that particular question, which makes me even more curious, but since that was like thousands of years ago, I've accepted that I'll never know the answer.

Martha has been teaching me all the rules in regards of what to do, what not to do, and what the mating rules are – as if I even want a mate, blah. She has told me about our weaknesses and our obvious strengths. Apparently the books and movies got the silver thing right, however it is more like an allergy rather than a death sentence. Of course too much silver will kill us, but let's be real too much of anything can kill ya. Martha says it is very important to know our history so I will know where it all comes from. Our history, I think with a snort, the pack children or cubs learn these lessons early on and here I am at 21 years of age learning the origins like a child, ugh.

Many times I have wondered if Martha would be insulted if I started banging my head against the desk? Dumb question, I know she will discipline the shit out of me. Deep breath in…and sigh.

Today Martha has invited several of the other pack females to the pack house. The pack house is an expansive three-story ranch style home with a full wrap-around porch. There are barns, stables, corrals, and even a traditional style bunkhouse if several of us need to crash here for the night. It is nestled in the high valleys along the western Montana mountains on over 500 acres of picturesque property. Normal people should be so lucky, I think to myself with a shake of my head as I put the pitchforks and shovels away.

I currently reside in the main house, which we affectionately call the pack house. I stay in one of the back bedrooms, mostly because I'm new and also because I'm, what's the word they've been calling me? Oh yeah, "unstable." Ha, if only they knew how unstable I really am.

Half the time I feel like a paranoid freak walking around on eggshells as I wait for her to appear and the other half of the time I'm trying to ignore her when she is around. I'm sure they all see me as a twitchy pup, ugh.

I never knew true fear before the night I was bitten, not this level of fear, now I carry it with me every day and if that makes me a little jumpy, then I guess I'm a little jumpy.

Side note because I know there are a lot of werewolf books out there so I just want to clear a few things up:

1) There are no overweight, out-of-shape werewolves. Our bodies are burning calories at such a high rate there is no way any of us could be heavy. We run, we work hard, we push each other hard when we practice combatives. Yeah, that's right I'm learning to fight like a champ 3 days a week, yee-haw cowboy! We as wolves are more than humans could ever hope to be. The men are usually a combination of bulging muscles and lean lines, and the females are the smaller version of that. When I was a human I was in shape, but now as a wolf I'm in crazy good shape. My body is stronger in all ways, and because of all the chores I do my skin is tan

and my muscles are toned. I am fit and I can honestly appreciate that little perk.

2) There are no fated mates or true mate crap. You find someone you want to be with, build a life with and you share a bite or two (little bit of unexplainable magic takes place) and then you're mated. For life! That's just a bit too intense for me right now, but kudos to those who wish to settle down and bring more pups into society.

3) The kids don't turn into werewolves as children. Call it a failsafe since children aren't very good at controlling their emotions and no way would werewolves stay hidden all these centuries if a child just turned into a wolf out of nowhere. So usually a young wolf turns for the first time between the ages of 18 to 25.

4) Oh and most importantly, werewolves don't go around biting humans. Do humans get attacked by lone wolves? Sure, but those humans never shift into wolves. So apparently I'm a rare case? Alpha Gregory is still

trying to figure out why this has happened to me and I appreciate his dedication, but I've accepted this is permanent at this point. The circumstances behind my attack and subsequent change have made several people in the pack suspicious and curious about if it was a pre-meditated attack. Great, chalk that up to one more thing to be paranoid about.

Right ok enough about the rules, back to being in the pack house, making breakfast with several other pack females, purebred females I might ad., I can feel the tension rise in the room by several degrees – we all can, the joy of all of us being wolves is we can sense pretty much anything from fear and anger to joy and desire, which makes for a ridiculous lack of privacy.

I know the tension isn't just because I'm new to the pack it's because I'm the outsider here, the mistake of nature that just shouldn't be. Contrary to the cult classics and popular belief, werewolves can wield some serious control – henceforth why I can actually keep from changing. However, none of my pack has ever heard of a non-purebred wolf being able to accomplish such a feat. Heck most of them haven't even met a non-pure like me. Such a joy being an anomaly in a new place, ha! Apparently having more human blood in my line means I should be weaker, not stronger. Hmm, good to know.

As werewolves we can become subject to our passions and anger can bring forth the wolf at ANY TIME. That's right, werewolves change at any time of the month, day or night. Freaky right? Meh, I find it pretty cool, but I'm still not giving into the wolf, not yet.

There are other werewolf rules, well laws really: We can date humans, but they are not allowed in the pack and they do not fall under pack protection, and we obviously cannot turn them or have children with them as our biological makeup doesn't match. Basically the old school view is humans are toys, enjoy them until you find your wolf mate. Which is another rule I can't believe, it is highly discouraged to sleep around with other wolves, but its alright to fool around with humans until you find your mate. Yeah, the hairy beasts actually have morals…of a sort.

I understand why Martha and her mate the alpha, Gregory, worry about me. For each day I refuse to give in to the impulse surging through me to change, is another that sees me tenser, and more on edge. I know I'm walking on a tight rope and soon, very soon that rope is going to snap. I'm no quitter. I'm going to fight tooth and nail to the bitter end, and it will be bitter for there is something I haven't told my pack – I see a ghost, the ghost of an eerie young girl who tells me I have to change into the wolf. Her voice grows more insistent each day and that voice makes my skin crawl. Three days after I was bitten she appeared to me, and three weeks after I was bitten I began to realize that little girl might not be a hallucination and she might not be a ghost either.

As the females keep chatting and putting together snacks for later this afternoon, I try to keep myself out of the way by keeping my head down and moving things as directed. I find myself going back over the last three months and how I've had to ask many innocently placed questions to figure out what was happening to me. What I found out was that little girl was no ghost, but a damn werewitch. Yeah that's right, a werewitch, which is something over half the pack believes to be a myth.

So how was I, newbie werewolf who was also a non-pure supposed to explain to my pack that a freakin' werewitch was constantly hanging around and persistently telling me to become a wolf? Yeah, I make a scoffing noise and quickly look around realizing I'm in a room with a bunch of female werewolves and I have no idea what they're talking about – what if I just insulted somebody? Nobody seems to be paying attention to me, but I'm not fooled, we have excellent hearing, so I know they're letting me be for some reason and I narrow my eyes in suspicion as I look from one female to another. They are definitely up to something and I can feel the tension roll through my shoulders. I bite my lip and try to slow my breathing down, to back down from the rage.

Martha notices my struggle and soon all the females do to as the room grows silent. "Lee, are you ok?" Martha asks quietly. I turn towards her, keeping my eyes down so as not to show a challenge, "Yes Martha." There are a few more seconds of quiet before everyone turns back to their tasks. I want to shout that I'm not ok, but a wispy figure catches my attention in the corner – she's back, the little girl is back and she's once again watching me with that eerie electric blue gaze of hers.

I learned a lot about werewitches from Maggie, a fairly low ranking 75 year old wolf – she only looks about 21 though. Maggie is from Ireland and she has many old school mystical beliefs that most of the other wolves don't share. She said that if a werewitch tells/asks/wants you to do something, there is a reason, a very BAD reason, so avoid it at all costs. So I took her advice and I'm avoiding changing into a wolf, but the cost of that decision is so high; I was beginning to lose pack support. Instead of having their sympathy because they thought I was scared to change, now I was getting their disgust because they thought I hated their kind. I know it is only a matter of time before the shit hits the fan.

Some of the pack may think Maggie is crazy, but she seems the most sane to me at this point. Course I'm seeing a werewitch, so maybe I'm just as freakin' nuts as her. Sigh. I push my hand through my hair, rubbing my temples as I try to sort it all out in my brain, but no matter what it all keeps circling into one big mess.

"Well hey there Shaw!" Kaley a younger wolf calls out as a male wolf comes into the kitchen and the wispy child disappears from the room.

Damn I think as I give him a glare, so that's what the ladies are up to….matchmaking.

Shaw is a fine-looking muscled brown wolf and he made the mistake of giving me a smooch about a month ago. I may have slashed his face with my claws; no not my nails, actual claws. Yeah, that's that whole anger thing I mentioned earlier, as well as me being on edge. I had to take several breaths to get myself back under control, while an equally amused and pissed of Shaw told me to, "Just change already." The urge to slice his throat had been a strong one as I spit out the next words, "Ah, I see, just trying to force the new girl eh? Piss off Shaw." Shaw had stared at me with those dark blue eyes and his lips had been set into a grim line before settling into a smirk. "Lee, if I wanted you force wouldn't be necessary." Before I could say something that would have totally gotten me into trouble he continues in a more serious tone, "Come on girl, you know you're on a hair trigger, so just change, become the wolf, and move on." I growled in response, crap I actually growled. I looked away from Shaw so I wouldn't have to see his smug look. Within seconds Maggie had come over and led me away – another classic babysitter moment. Ugh. I feel my cheeks heat up from the memory, I'm still so ashamed.

Shaw may be good looking with all those lean muscles and curly sandy brown hair, but he sure can be a pain. At over 6 feet tall, he's about the same height as the other male wolves, but there's something about him, something different. Believe it or not, I actually consider him a friend now. He tries to get me to change, but he also backs off when I ask him too. He neither hates me or seems to like me at least not like that, and I feel safe around him knowing that, but I'm so not thrilled about this matchmaking business.

So I try to get out of there ASAP. "Martha, may I be excused to get my books for class?"

The whole room goes still as the females realize I'm not sticking around for their little scheme, "Sure Lee, but we'll talk more later."

"Of course," I say with a nod and before leaving I catch Shaw's stare – he looks like he's holding in a laugh, so I decide to toy with him a bit as I know he doesn't want a mate any more than I do, "Looking good Shaw," I say with a wink and it effectively wipes the smile off his face.

Before exiting the room completely I see the women look at Shaw and I hear him stutter something about going outside to check on the chores I did. I can't keep it in, so I laugh my way down the hall, smiling as I hear the distant laughter of the other women.

Chapter 2

Werewolf 101

LEE

Today in class (haha) I'm learning more about werewolf history and the pack structure. I've spent the last three months learning this crap...ok in all fairness it's not crap and it is actually pretty interesting stuff, but it also reminds me of all I've lost. The other wolves don't have this issue because they are born into pack life and they grow up knowing where they've come from and where they're going. But me? I was a human once, I had friends back home, a life, and that life I had before just doesn't get erased because of one bite. I remember all those I've had to leave behind in order to protect those in my new life. I'm happy to protect them and I know that is partly due to the pack mentality, but I miss home and at times I miss the simplicity of being a human.

I had to completely disconnect from everyone I had ever known soon after I left the hospital...its like I dropped off the face of the earth, and yet I haven't, I'm right here.

I understand history is important, history is part of who we are and it guides who we will become. I understand why it is especially important to the purebloods because they can trace their heritage back centuries, but for a newbie like me the pack structure is most important because if I don't show the right respect to the right wolf, well I end up flying across a room or in a fur-flying fight including teeth and claws. Yep, sucks to be the newbie in a wolf pack.

To recap a bit of what I learned, here we go:

Gregory is the current Alpha of our pack and is obviously mated to Martha the alpha female, he took over from Hal about 40 years ago. Hal is what we refer to as an old-timer because he is over 300 years old. His mate died centuries ago and he never re-mated, which left him childless. When an alpha has no sons he has no one to pass the alpha position down to, which can cause instability and in-fighting as the younger males fight for the position. Hal did not want this, but it had to happen.

Hal took in Gregory and his younger cousin Petroff, when they emigrated from Russia over 50 years ago. From what I understand the packs over there are a bit more vicious and there's more in-fighting for control. Makes me glad I was born in America. Gregory had to fight for the position of alpha when Hal decided to step down. I'm happy I wasn't around for that because alpha fights can get vicious as they can be fought to the death.

Hal still lives around the local area. He moved to the outskirts of Big Springs into a small house on a 20 acre wooded plot. He seems to enjoy life outside the pack. I've met him several times – he has so much wisdom to pass along, and even though he looks so young, he's like everyone's grandfather. Go figure.

Ok, focusing back on the facts I've learned. Both Gregory and Petroff are over 6 feet tall with muscular builds, however Petroff is a leaner version of Gregory. They both have trademark good looks and sea-green eyes. Men should not be that gorgeous, just saying. I'm talking sigh-worthy good looking, but they're not my type. That over-the-top alpha crap is insane and Martha is a far better woman than I am. I'm not saying I don't like Gregory, as a leader he is awesome, but I would never want him or Petroff as mates, no way.

Petroff could easily be an alpha in another 20 years or so, so I wouldn't be surprised to see him break off and either start a pack of his own or take over a pack from a weaker alpha. He has become quite a loner since his mate died back in Russia, so I don't see much of that guy.

Werewolf 101 has not only taught me who is related to whom, but also what each pack member looks like in their wolf forms. Naturally I would know all this if I had ever shifted and joined them on runs, but that's an argument I'm not going to address here. Our alpha and his cousin are gray and black wolves with blue eyes, which I shall remember if I'm ever walking in the woods alone.

The pack consists of over 50 individuals and its constantly growing. Some of the wolves are mated and/or married and some aren't. The children range from infants to teenagers, and I'm still trying to remember all the names, ages, and birthdays involved.

I find myself exasperated as Martha goes further down in the pack structure, "How do you remember everyone?" I ask with frustration.

Martha pauses in her lecture and smiles at me, "Lee, I'm over 135 years old and I was born and raised in this pack, of course I remember everyone. It's like

you and where you were from. You remember the
mailman there and the café owner, someday it will be
like that for you here. Just give it time." I nod as I realize
she's right, it took me my whole life to have everyone
memorized back home – I grew up with them, now I
need to grow with the people here. I take a deep breath
and then continue drawing out a family tree on my
notebook paper. Hey, I need a cheat sheet because
otherwise I may not figure this out for another five
years.

Martha and I take a break for lunch and I do a
few chores around the house. Most of the wolves are
clean freaks, which actually surprises me because
wolves in the wild seem slobby? I don't know, its just a
surprise how OCD they can all be about cleanliness,
however if I had 50 or more people circling in and out of
my house I would be a clean freak too…which is what is
happening. I was never a real messy person, but I'm
even more neat and organized now. I don't want to be

obsessed with cleanliness, so I'm hoping that particular trait stays with the purebloods.

We usually take a lunch break and then pick back up on the studying about 2pm and Martha will quiz me about what I've learned about werewolf history. She'll ask me about the origins of werewolves in Russia, Europe, the Viking era (yeah that was a fun fact to learn), and why our breed started emigrating to North America. She'll also ask me how many alphas are in Canada and the U.S. and what their names are. She has quizzed me so much in the last few months that I'm beginning to feel like I'm in college all over again.

"You need to know these things Lee," Martha presses me, "Outsiders will expect a wolf your age to know all about this and if wolves from other packs were to approach you, you don't want to make the mistake of inadvertently insulting them."

I sigh, "I know Martha, it's…it's just a lot to take in." She reaches across the table and squeezes my hand, "It'll be ok, we'll get you there."

Martha is so wonderful and patient. She has shown me werewolves can be gentle, kind, and patient. I would do anything for her and her children. Martha and Gregory have three wonderful kids; Annabelle, Viviana, and Eddie. Eddie may only be 7 years old, but he already shows an alpha's mentality. I hope he emulates his father as he gets older.

I shake my head to dispel these thoughts as I focus on Martha talking about other members of our pack like Shaw, Liam, Kelly, and Maggie. These are wolves I interact with a lot more than the others as they tend to be on babysitting duty, so to know details about them is good. I've had ups and downs with all the wolves in the pack, but it is getting better…slowly, but surely better. It can't possibly get worse, but aren't those supposed to be famous last words?

Liam and Kelly are another mated pair in the pack. Liam is a redhead with hazel eyes and has the typical lumberjack build, makes sense considering he's a carpenter. His wolf is brown, but there's a tinge of red in his fur and his gold eyes seem more yellow than the other wolves' eyes. Kelly is a trauma nurse and carries a bit of that intensity with her all the time. Her dishwater blonde hair is almost always in a bun and her pale blue eyes are older than her 25 years. Her wolf has golden eyes and is mottled colored, which makes her quite unique. Liam and Kelly grew up in this pack together; they went from childhood playmates to real mates, kind of adorable really.

I mentioned a bit about Maggie earlier, she's 75 years old, also a redhead, but her hair is not the same shade as Liam's as her curls are dark, almost an auburn. Her chocolate colored brown eyes always seemed to be filled with a little mischief, which matches her Irish heritage. She came over from Ireland around 20 years ago to avoid an unwanted mating and Gregory took her in. Maggie doesn't talk about that time of her life very much, but any time a new male wolf comes into the area she hides out for a few days. Best I can figure is she's worried the wolf she was supposed to mate has tracked her down. Personally, I think she likes her would-be mate, but the idea of commitment sent her running, but what do I know?

Oh, and I should mention the pack Beta, who is also the 2nd in command after Gregory. I personally would have thought it would have been Petroff, but like I said earlier, he's been messed up since his mate died. So, the current beta is a big ox of a man named William, but everyone calls him Bill. Bill is easily 6 feet 4 inches and has arms like tree trunks. His mate Shelby is actually older than him by about 35 years, now that's a cougar, I think with a laugh. They make a good couple; where Bill is more serious, Shelby is more playful. Bill has a rugged handsomeness about him with his dark brown hair and eyes. Shelby makes me think of a California girl with her pale blonde waist-length hair and

twinkly blue eyes. She is Barbie doll gorgeous, but she
is no ditz. Shelby is a lawyer and a damn fine one at that,
which compliments Bill's job on the police force. Bill is
a gray wolf with golden eyes and Shelby is a very
unusual white wolf with blue eyes. She's beautiful in
both forms, so many of us are jealous. They both accept
pack responsibility so easily I actually find myself
envious. I struggle with the restrictions of being a wolf
and the pressure of always putting the pack first. It's not
easy, but I'm trying.

Martha stays with her kids for a bit after we've
cleaned up the lunch dishes. I know she values time with
her children and I like to give her a little space during
that time, so I usually head back to the makeshift
classroom and study my notes. I think all of this
information is some pretty neat stuff, but some of it is a
little mundane. Do I want to know about everybody's
birthdays and anniversaries? Not really, but that's being
in a family so I'm gonna do my best to learn it.

I feel a slight chill go through the room and I know who it is, I always know when it's her.

"What do you want?" I growl as the wispy form of the werewitch appears and stands in front of the board Martha writes things down on. I said it was Werewolf Class 101, so of course there is a chalk board. I look to the door, and luckily Martha is stalled in the kitchen with the kids.

"Don't be nasty," she says in the innocent voice only a child can muster. I would say she's roughly 11 years old, but she seems older somehow. She looks over her shoulder, perusing the information still on the board. "History huh?" she asks, but I don't answer, so she looks back at me.

"Yes, I'm learning werewolf history, ok? Now can you please go?"

"You know, I could teach you a thing or two about history. I know way more about the old ways than any wolf you'll ever meet."

I won't lie, I'm tempted. Who wouldn't want to know about how things really were back then?

"You know about the old ways?" I say with some skepticism, "How old are you little werewitch?"

"Too young to be what I am, and too old to ever be young again," she says with so much wisdom and sadness I actually feel a bit of compassion for her.

I think over her answer about her age - is it a riddle or does she really believe that about her life? Is this all a game to her? I don't know, but I want to know more.

"What's your history then?" I ask feeling equal parts curious and anxious as I can hear the kids settling down in the kitchen; Martha will be back soon.

"Well," she says with a small smile and I see her twirling some white strands of her hair around her delicate little fingers, "I was born to a Viking." She giggles as she sees my shock and then she's gone.

Martha walks back into the room and I try to wipe the shock from my features because what would I say? Hey Martha a little girl werewitch with eerie blue eyes and long white hair just told me she's so old she came from the Viking era?!? Umm no!

I mean what the hell? How has she not aged any older than her preteen years? How has she lived this long all by herself? Wait, does she live by herself? I think it over as Martha makes a comment, yes I think the little girl does…she has that sadness, that loneliness about her that she has to be a loner.

"Lee are you listening?"

I break out of my thoughts and do my best to focus, "Sorry, yes Martha I am paying attention," and for the rest of the afternoon I try to because the next bit is quite important.

Martha explains the whole 'werewolf aging' thing to me. I mean I had figured some of it out because Hal may be over 300 years old, but he only looks about

65. So basically we age slowly, ok cool. She also says that's why we tend not to interact so much with humans in one specific area because they are eventually going to notice we don't age very fast. Even the most clueless human is going to find that weird. It has me wondering if I've ever met a werewolf back east and never knew it?

Probably.

When Martha asks if I have any questions, at first I want to say no because I want to get out of the classroom as fast as possible and get on one of the laptops to look up anything in the Viking era that might help me pinpoint the identity of this girl or some kind of information. But then I realize…why not just ask Martha?

"Yeah, umm, could you tell me a little bit more about the Viking era? I know you mentioned some small things before, but did they believe in the more mystical side of things?"

As soon as I say the word 'mystical' I know I've gone too far, especially considering the way Martha is looking at me right now.

"Mystical? Lee what do you mean?"

"Umm, never mind," I decide chickening out is the best way to go.

"Alright let's call it quits for the day then," Martha's words bring a sigh of relief to my lips, a sigh that is short lived as she adds "Gotta get ready for combatives."

"Crap," I mumble, which only makes Martha chuckle as I close up my notebook. Its going to be hours before I can look up anything about Vikings. Some frustration builds inside me, but I can't afford to be ruled by emotions right now, so combatives it is.

I find myself enjoying the combative training because it helps with the tension I feel from my refusal to shift, but it sucks getting my butt handed to me three times a week because the other wolves are faster and better. Its not like I'm super weak, I could totally kick a human's butt no problem...even if they were a huge man in super good shape. I may be shorter than the other wolves, but I am equally as strong as them, however these purebloods happen to have a lifetime of training under their belts and I'm still learning. I'll get there though, one whooping at a time.

I feel myself grow determined as I change from my t-shirt and blue jean shorts into some comfortable black workout clothes. "Deep breath Lee," I tell myself, "The pain only lasts a short while." I shake my head to clear out the cobwebs and then head outside to join about 20 or so packmates for training. It's go time.

WEREWITCH

I smile a little as I watch Lee struggle to learn about her pack. She seems to be adjusting as well as a human can to werewolf life. Hmm, I had a pack once, well a family really because I wasn't always a werewolf.

I try to remember my mother's face…blonde hair, green eyes, long braids mixed in amongst her long straight hair. I try, but it's been too long, I cannot really picture her at all and the thought makes me sad.

I should not have had to live this long without my mother I think sadly. I regret the pain I've put Lee through, but I need her and I'm so close, so close. I hear Martha, one of the kindest women I've ever known in my time, rattle off some more facts and my good mood is quickly restored, but again it turns bitter as she talks with such pride about the history of the pack and of werewolves in general.

A bunch of nonsense is what it is. I wonder how proud all the wolves would be if they knew what I knew about "our history." Werewolves were around long before my time and there is no pride in how they came to be. Let me share the tale I was raised with, the truth of our history that none now would ever believe.

In the time when people believed in Queen Mab and Merlin, a time without a known God, there was a man, a good looking but selfish man who wanted for his wife a woman so beautiful none could compare. He brought her all manner of gifts and promised her a castle to live in, but still she refused saying her father had promised her to another. In his rage he killed the beautiful young woman. Immediately upon her death, the woman's mother arrived and she cursed the man to the life of a beast for she was a witch with much power. However, Nature always finds a balance of its own and it found own for such a dark curse. The price for the witch's curse was high, higher than she could have ever fathomed. Now the witch also had a son who had a daughter of his own. This daughter had the blood of a witch running through her veins. The daughter was young, just into her teens when she was bitten by the beast her grandmother had created. The grandmother mourned for the cursed life her granddaughter would have to live. She tried to reverse the curse upon the man, but she was only able to tweak the curse allowing the man to live as both man and beast. Nature decided to be kind to the woman in return and allowed the granddaughter to also live as man and beast, but because of the witch's blood the granddaughter became something more than the man, she became a werewitch. A cursed being that must walk the world alone, forever immortal, full of extreme power, and unable to have a mate of her own.

The witch was grateful for Nature's kindness, but saddened by the lonely life her granddaughter was cursed to live. Her granddaughter was cast out from the village she had grown up in as fear of her power spread. She indeed had to live a long lonely life, but because she was so kind, Nature again decided to step in. Nature allowed the granddaughter an escape from the life her grandmother had inadvertently cursed her to, but that freedom comes with a dark price. She paid the price, albeit sorrowfully, and other werewitches have paid that price. A price I have yet to pay and as I focus my gaze on Lee, I see the price and I long for it.

Chapter 3

Fist To Cuffs

LEE

A punch to the jaw has my head spinning sideways and unleashing a low grumbled, "Dammit." Maggie's brown eyes are dancing at me as I smell blood and touch the spot where she hit. Split lip, nice.

"C'mon Lee, you should be getting quicker at this," she mocks at me as I rub my now sore jaw.

Dozens of other wolves have paired up and we've all spread out in the huge backyard. Everyone is wearing basic workout clothes and tennis shoes, which is nice because a steel-toed boot kick to the body is really unpleasant.

Each pair is running through the basics in the large backyard and everyone's doing good at blocking punches, well everyone except me it seems. I can't predict every move Maggie is going to make and even though my reflexes are fast I haven't spent my whole life being trained to do combatives.

"I am quicker," I fire back at her as I fake a punch with my left fist and surprise her by striking her left knee with my right foot. I hear a small crunch and I know I've done a little damage.

"Oww!" she yells out, and as I relax and let loose a chuckle I miss seeing her charge me with her head lowered.

"Oompf," is the only sound I let out as her head lands into my stomach. I land on my back, hard, knocking the air out of me with a whoosh. I'm struggling hard now as Maggie's fists rain punches on my face. I reach up and hook my right arm around the back of her neck, pulling her down on top of me so her fists won't do so much damage. I'm 100% sure I'm going to lose this fight, but I'm going to go out kicking.

Sure enough within seconds Maggie lands a solid punch along my ribs, no doubt cracking a few and I lose my grip on her neck. She breaks free of my arm and I roll quickly to the left trying to escape her before she can inflict more damage. I may be a werewolf and we may heal super-fast, but that doesn't mean we can't feel pain. I can tell I'm going to be sore for the rest of the night.

She lands a few more punches before she backs off and I'm struggling to stand as my cracked ribs make me want to wheeze. "You're right, you are getting better. Soon I'll have to be more careful." We both chuckle a bit because that may not sound like a compliment, but in our world it is.

"Why did you have to go for my ribs?" I complain as I try to catch a solid breath.

"Meh," she shrugs her shoulders and tosses her hair over her shoulder, "It's not like you're going for a run tonight with the pack, so why not?"

I roll my eyes, "Gee thanks, good to know. Not like adding more pressure to shift."

Her eyes narrow at me as her face grows serious, "You know I'd never do that Lee."

I immediately regret what I said, "Yeah I know Maggie, sorry I said that. Guess I'm just feeling frustrated with everything."

Maggie never stays serious for long, I don't know if it has to do with her Irish heritage or what, so she nods back with a smile, "No worries kiddo." She laughs as I roll my eyes in mock exasperation at the nickname and her Irish lilt. Maggie is something else.

"SWITCH!" Bill calls out and Maggie heads off to her left. The way the group is set up is into 2 circles; one inner circle, these partners don't move when we have to switch and an outer circle that rotates – giving each person a chance to spar with several wolves in one setting. Usually the young wolves are in the inner circle, I happen to be among that group because I have so little experience.

I'm hoping my next sparring partner will be Kelly because I know she'll take it easy on my ribs. Sometimes it pays to spar with a person in the medical profession. No such luck for me though as Kelly is called over to check a younger wolf's bloody face on the other side of the circle. I look to see who's up next for me and my eyes take in an all too familiar figure…Shaw. Damn is the only word that goes through my mind as our eyes meet and his mouth turns into a playful smirk.

Shaw continues to smile at me as he moves into position, his dark blue eyes seem to be twinkling – he's got to be up to something. Even though we've become friends of a sort, I still want to punch that smirk right off his good looking face.

"BEGIN," Bill calls out and the next round of sparring begins. I don't even get a chance before Shaw has me on the ground. I take a swing, but he catches my wrist before it meets its mark and then he quickly grabs my other wrist.

Shaw now has my arms pinned to the ground above my head, which of course pushes my breasts up to graze against his hard chest and his legs are lying between mine instead of straddling my waist – that's his mistake. I know it's all a tease for him as he's trying to amp me up because after that first time of me slashing his face when he gave me a smooch he's been way better behaved.

I know he's just being playful, so when I shimmy my hips in return he arches his eyebrow. Poor poor male, he doesn't know I was on the dance team in high school and this chick has flexibility like no other. I bend by legs back towards my shoulders causing his weight to settle onto me. I feel a painful twinge in my ribs, but I ignore it; I'm not losing this opportunity to blindside

Shaw. I can tell I'm distracting him, so I smile and bat my eyelashes, which finally makes him suspicious, but it's too late. I hook my legs over his biceps and use the strength in my legs to pin his arms to his sides and begin pounding into his face with my fists. He lets loose a muffled curse, but no way am I letting up while I have the advantage.

The satisfaction I feel when I see blood trickle from his lip is enormous and I have to suppress a cackle as my punches connect with his face a few more times before he finally frees himself from my leg lock and we roll away from each other. I know he won't take it easy on me now, the man has his pride after all, but no matter the beating I'm sure to receive the look on his face as I tricked him was totally worth it.

We both stand up and Shaw isn't smirking now. Oh he's not in a bad mood, but he isn't trying to play with me anymore either.

"That was a good move Lee," he says with a tinge of respect in his voice.

"Thanks," I puff out as my ribs are still in the process of healing, "Maggie told me when in doubt use your sexuality to beat the guys."

To my surprise he laughs, "As long as you're only using it on me, I don't mind." I roll my eyes and shake my head as he winks at me before he sweeps his leg around and drops me on my rear. I spring back up…in time to meet his leg as it slams into my upper thigh. Down I go again. I use my hands to slap away his punches as I struggle to get up from my knees.

"Nice kick," I say through gritted teeth as I half stand up. I'm only barely able to deflect his next kick which grazes the ribs Maggie already gave a pounding too. I try to land a few kicks and punches of my own, but Shaw easily blocks them all. He moves with the ease of a skilled fighter and I try not to let that get to me as I remind myself I'm still learning.

He catches my fist a mere inch from his face and uses it to spin me around and pin my arm behind my back. I look up at him over my shoulder, "Shaw that hurts," I say in a whiny voice, but I can tell he's not falling for it this time, so I use my right foot to stomp on his right instep, his breath leaves him in a hiss as his body lurches. His head is lower than it should be and I can't help but use my head to slam back into his nose. I can't quite describe the noise that comes out of his mouth as blood trickles down his face, nor am I prepared for when he flips me over and lands more punches to my ribs. I hear a few more of them crack before Bill calls out for us to stop.

"Ass," I murmur quietly as both Shaw and I catch our breath.

He smiles back at me, "You deserved it with that nose smash sweetheart." I'd like to be mad at him, but I'm not. Shaw is a pretty fun guy and when all is said and done he didn't take it easy on me after that first trick

I pulled and I appreciate that. I don't want to be coddled and he knows that.

"I had to up the ante, you were still being too gentle."

"Oh so you like it rough eh?" he says, wiggling his eyebrows at me suggestively as he wipes the blood off his face.

"That's not what I meant and you know it," I mockingly grumble back, trying not to laugh as I keep a hand over my sore ribs. Yep definitely going to be sore until tomorrow, I think as I take a few more shaky breaths. Is it selfish to want to be able to heal even faster?

"Do I?" Shaw smirks at me before heading off to his next sparring partner. I find myself smiling as I watch him move off, what a guy.

I get Shelby next and I know I'm going to take a beating…so make that my ribs are going to be sore until tomorrow evening.

Shelby gives me all she's got, she has to as mate to the beta and I don't even come close to doing any significant damage. Best thing I can do is keep up a decent defense until her mate Bill tells us to stop.

When Bill finally ends the round I'm not even on my feet. Sure Shelby is sweating from the exertion she put in to kicking my ass, but I'm lying on my back in the grass just staring up at the sky as the pain in my ribs has now reached a crescendo.

"You good?" Shelby asks even though we both know the answer to that.

"Sure," I say weakly, "Just give me a few and I'll be on my feet in no time."

Shelby shakes her head at my weak announcement and reaches down to help me up,

"C'mon." I know wolves are full of pride, but I allow her support without hesitation and she helps me limp over to one of the picnic tables in the backyard. If I had been planning to go out for the pack run tonight there'd be no way I could go now. Sure I could have run once my wolf started healing up my ribs, but I wouldn't have been able to keep up with the group, good thing I don't do the shifting business…not yet anyway.

Not yet, that's what I keep telling myself because I do want to shift, so badly I can practically taste it, but its not safe. I hope my inner wolf understands that. I just need to figure this werewitch thing out first and then, then I can shift and enjoy the freedom of the wolf. My inner wolf gives out a yip inside my head and I smile at her excitement. Yep, one day we'll be free. But right now I just need to take nice and easy breaths because the pain from my ribs makes me feel like I might die.

I know our fighting sounds vicious, but considering how fast we heal it's really nothing. Shaw's nose stopped bleeding within seconds of me actually injuring it. My ribs started healing the second they were cracked. We don't heal instantly, but we do start the healing process as soon as we're injured. In our wolf form we heal even faster, so the young wolf from earlier that Kelly checked on shifted into his animal form and now he's doing fine.

I was never about fighting before my werewolf life, never had a reason to be. I was from a small town and then attended a pretty safe college. I wasn't stupid, I knew people got attacked, but it wasn't until after Jeannie and I got attacked in the mountains that I supported fighting, more specifically self-defense. It's good to know how to defend oneself, never know when another rogue wolf will come out of the shadows or if a man will get a little too handsy. I want to be able to protect myself, although when I think of handsy the mental image that comes to mind is one of Shaw pinning my arms over my head…and I don't find myself getting too irritated by it.

Chapter 4

Going For A Night's Run

LEE

After sparring we all take turns getting cleaned up, some in the pack house and others use the showers in the bunk house. Showering may seem pointless as most of the adult pack members are going for a run tonight after dinner, but just because we're wolves doesn't mean we don't like to be clean.

I would like to say the pack trusts me to watch over the cubs all by myself while they're out running through the woods, but that would be an obvious lie. I am one of the ones being babysat afterall, yep, feels good. Not.

My irritation rises slightly as I finish up with my shower. I don't want them to see me as a child! I want them to see me as an equal, as someone who will do the right thing. I pause in toweling my hair dry as I realize to my surprise I want to earn their respect and trust. I want to be seen as a positive not a negative.

What is happening to me?

Is it just the increasing sense of pack mentality?

Or do I genuinely want these people to like me?

Both.

That's the resounding word that goes through my mind as I pull a baggy black shirt over my black and blue skin knowing a tight shirt will just irritate my ribs more. A loose pair of gray sweatpants are soon to follow. Ah yes, comfort I think with a small groan before grabbing a brush & trying to run it through my hair as quickly as possible, easier said than done right now though. Several minutes later I head down the hall to rejoin the pack for dinner.

As I get nearer to my pack members I think it over more and acknowledge that I do want their trust and respect. I want them to realize I would never hurt any of the children, but I can also recognize that's hard to believe when I'm the person walking around on a hair trigger.

I may hate being babysat and made to feel like a child, but when I look at the pack cubs I smile seeing their youthful exuberance; there's just something about kids that's fun to be around. Maybe having to stay in tonight isn't the worst thing to happen, maybe I need this more than I first believed.

I move into the kitchen to help with dinner because even though I'm injured there's still a job to be done. With a majority of the pack here…it's a lot of food that's going to be consumed and I'm glad we did some of the prep work earlier.

"Just shift and you'll heal faster," a young teenage wolf tells me. I look away from the kids and scan the young wolf's features…I've seen her around, but I'm not sure of her name. "I'm not shifting," I respond to her statement. She stares at me for a few seconds before shrugging her shoulders and turning back to the counter to cut up more veggies for the salad. Yes, even though we're werewolves we do enjoy a good salad, shocking I know.

I grab a knife and start slicing up some cucumbers as the smell of steaks being grilled reaches my nose through the open kitchen window. Mmm, smells tasty and I can practically feel myself drooling. What wolf doesn't love steak? C'mon now.

Later that night after everyone has been fed and cleanup has occurred the adult wolves get ready to go for a night run. The sun has set, but there is still a hint of light in the sky. The cubs are inside the living room watching a movie and several teenage wolves are watching over the young ones. Meanwhile I'm standing near the back door with the lights off, peering through one of the big windows along the closed in porch.

Yeah I know I sound a bit like a creeper, but I'm not.

Everything in me longs to join my packmates out there as they begin to shift into their wolf forms. It isn't painful for them and they change in such a graceful way that I consider it to be one of the most beautiful things to behold. It gets me every time I see it happen. Smooth skin becomes fur, hands and feet become paws, and the eyes, the eyes glow with an inner fire no human eyes could ever show. Again, it is truly a beautiful thing to behold.

I feel my own wolf come forward inside me and I know my eyes are no longer human. My brown eyes have faded away and the blue irises of my wolf are at the forefront. She wants her freedom and I wish I could give it to her. As my packmates finish shifting and start to run towards the tree line yipping and cavorting as if they are pups, one brown wolf holds back from the pack. The wolf instead looks back towards the house and I feel his golden eyes connect with mine.

"Shaw," his name slips out before I can stop it and the sound of my voice snaps me from the trance I've been in. I take a step back, putting myself further into the darkness of the back porch hoping it hides me from his eyes. Shaw hears me, I know he does and he lets out a bark before turning and chasing off after the pack. My heart is racing and I want to follow, but I can't. I close my eyes trying to push the wolf back down and I can feel it destroy me a little bit more as I refuse to let her out. I open my now brown eyes as I feel a tear roll down my cheek. "I'm sorry," I whisper to my wolf as I wipe the tear away. I hear her mournful howl in my head and it cuts at me even more as I acknowledge the pain I'm putting us both through.

I fall asleep that night with thoughts of wolves running through the woods in my head. I'm hoping the good thoughts will keep the nightmares away because I'm starting to be afraid to fall asleep. She comes for me in my dreams now, the little werewitch. For the first two months she only bothered me in the daylight hours, but now even in my sleep I can find no peace, not that I had much before after Jeannie's death.

I drift off with the hope she won't be there this time, but again I am wrong…

I'm not sleeping in my bed at the ranch instead I'm back up in the mountains near Glacier National Park; it's cold and I can see my breath as it fogs in front of me. The cold stings my cheeks, but I have no scarf to wrap around my exposed face, nor a coat to pull over my bare arms. I've never been here in the cold before, the last time it was early summer and Jeannie was there. I look behind me, trying to peer into the darkness, but I see nothing when suddenly I hear a twig snap. I spin my head back around and there is Jeannie. She's looking back at me with a smile on her face telling me some joke or other and even though she's alive and happy, I can't stop the sense of dread that fills me.

"Jeannie RUN!" I scream, but it's too late, again and again I try, but again and again I'm too late. A huge branch appears in my hands and no matter how hard I swing it the beast won't let my friend go.

The attack happens all over again, but this time the wolf shifts after killing Jeannie and it's the werewitch smiling at me as blood drips from her young lips.

"You!" I cry out in shock. "Why?" I demand as I swing the tree branch around trying to hit her.

"Because I need you," she whispers back.

"For what?" I scream in anger and pain as I keep swinging the branch at her to no avail. She is so quick, so agile that she easily escapes every swing I send her way.

An evil smile comes across her innocent young face, "For this!" she cries before plunging her hand into my chest. Her cold fingers squeeze around my heart and I can feel it starting to slow. My arms still and the branch drops to the ground as I feel a weakness enter me. I look at her in horror as the pure agony of her touch seeps into my veins and a cold like no other fills my chest. My mouth opens wide and I scream as the oncoming darkness descends.

I wake up with my scream of terror still ringing in my ears and my hand clutches the area above my heart. My eyes search out every corner of the room looking for the threat and my ears are peeled for any sound. No one seems to be up, so my screams must have only been in my head. My heart is pounding, oh thank goodness it is still pounding.

I realize it was only a nightmare, but I can still feel her hand around my heart. I place my hand more tightly against my chest trying to dispel that sick feeling of having my heart squeezed by those cold fingers. Shivers run down my arms and I look around the darkened room again and then again trying to find any hint of the werewitch's presence, but there is nothing. Everything is in its place. The door is closed and the windows are shut, but did I really think she would leave a trail? No.

I breathe deeply trying to calm myself, forgetting momentarily about my sore ribs causing myself to hunch over in pain. I know there'll be no more sleep tonight so I get up, gather some clothes together, and quietly head down the hall to the bathroom.

I still feel a chill along my skin as I splash cold water on my face, shocking myself more awake from the nightmare I just had. "You're safe, you're safe." That's what I tell myself as I look in the mirror. The words that I have said over and over the last few months no longer seem to work…because with every day that passes I know I'm less and less safe.

I stare at myself in the mirror and I can see the weariness in my face, the small shadows that are forming beneath my eyes. "You're losing it Lee, you're fucking losing it, so get your shit together because she's just waiting for you to fail." I speak quietly, but fiercely, trying to find every ounce of motivation I have left. I hear a creak down the hallway, and I clamp my lips shut. With wolves in the house one never knows just how much privacy one has. I wait a few heartbeats more, but when I hear nothing else I let out a quiet breath. I shake my head to dispel my anxiety, however it lingers around me like a dark cloud. Will I never be free of this nightmare? My inner wolf consoles me with a yip and a panting smile. I have not given her the freedom she so desperately desires, yet still she is with me. "Thank you," I whisper to her as I wrap my arms around my body – giving myself the hug I so dearly need.

I take a hot shower which helps rid some of the cold I still feel within me. I quickly throw on a pair of light blue jeans and a faded green sweater that has seen better days. I gather my black hair up in a ponytail and leave my room, intending to head out to the barns and get started on chores early...real early if the time on my bedroom clock was anything to go by.

I head outside a bit lost in my thoughts when the sound of the back door creaking open has me spinning around and crouching low to the ground. So low my jean covered knees brush against the wet grass. Guess those combatives have been really paying off because I'm ready for the incoming attack.

"Where you going Lee?" Shaw's softly voiced question has me feeling a bit foolish so I stand up quickly and try to act more casual. I look him over; my heightened sight picks out even the small details. He's wearing his typical blue jeans and boots, but instead of a white t-shirt he has on a dark red long-sleeve shirt. Guess he's starting to feel the chill of the late summer as well. His hair looks slightly mussed as if he just woke up, his eyes though... his eyes are steady, just watching me. I blink a few times looking away from him, but my eyes keep getting drawn back to his.

"Got the short straw for babysitter duty did you?" I deflect, trying to severe whatever connection is happening between us right now.

"No." he pauses before continuing, "We don't keep tabs on you 24/7 you know, plus we figured you'd sleep well tonight with your ribs being so sore."

"Well obviously I couldn't sleep Shaw, so I'm heading out to do some chores. Clear my head, no big deal," I finish with a shrug of my shoulders. I'm trying to be casual as I don't want him to pick up on my anxiety, but I'm pretty certain that I'm failing.

We stare at each other for a few moments more and his midnight blue eyes seem to be searching my soul. It makes me uncomfortable in a way I can't explain so I turn away. Now in most werewolf books this is where the more dominant wolf would freak out and demand some respect, but this isn't some cheesy werewolf story and Shaw isn't that big of a jerk. He knows I mean no disrespect, so instead of pulling some dominant wolf crap…he follows me.

"Do you dream about your friend's death?" Shaw asks me as I reach the small door on the near side of the barn.

I freeze, my hand still on the metal latch as I'm momentarily getting thrown back into my nightmare and Jeannie's never ending screams.

"That and other things," I answer back before swinging the door wide, flipping on the light switch and stepping into the barn. Shaw and I gather up a couple of tools and the wheelbarrows, saying nothing and walking down the aisles. It is still too early to let the horses out, but we can at least clear out the hay bags and water buckets in each stall.

"I'm here if you need to talk about it Lee," his statement has me setting down the wheelbarrow to turn around and face him. I scan his face and what I see has me sucking in a breath. He's not mocking or joking around, no this time he's serious and there's a depth of emotion in those eyes I can't quite name.

"Thanks Shaw. I don't know if I'll ever go to sleep and not dream about Jeannie dying," I suck in a breath as I say that, not wanting to break down in front of him. Once I feel steady again I push onwards, "But thanks. As for the other stuff…well I doubt you'd believe me."

"Try me," he coaxes gently as he raises his hand. I stiffen, unsure what he is about to do. He notices my reaction and his lips turn up in a small smile as his fingers reach along my cheek to tuck some of my loose hair behind my ear. His smile spreads at the taken aback expression on my face, "I'm not just about combatives you know. I'm here to listen." His gentleness both surprises me and makes me want to share everything with him. I'm tired of hiding everything and doubting my decision to keep this werewitch stuff quiet, but when I open my mouth…nothing comes out. I shrug my shoulders and shake my head.

"I can't Shaw, I just can't," I say not bothering to hide the emotion from my voice.

"Someday you will," he says with such confidence it makes me smile. He smiles back before nodding his head towards the untouched stalls, "Let's get back to work babe."

"Don't call me babe," I say as I turn around, hiding my smile from him. We continue on this way and finish a dozen other chores before any of the other pack members come down to the barn.

Amongst the comfortable silence we've been working in for the last few hours, Shaw suddenly starts speaking. He doesn't ask me any questions; he just talks in a quiet, gentle tone. He tells me about his childhood, how wonderful it was living without electricity and running water. A thing I cannot even fathom outside of camping for a weekend. Camping, crap don't think about camping, so I forcefully turn my mind back to Shaw's stories.

How old is he again? I find myself thinking back to Martha's classes and wondering if she ever mentioned his age...I don't think she has. If Shaw's childhood was in the early-1900s, then he's at least a hundred. Wow. Wow, is all my brain can process as I listen to more of his stories from a time I cannot even relate to.

He says he misses being young and having no real cares.

Huh, I thought he had no cares now. He seems so carefree and full of fun, but his next story opens a window for me to his private world...a window that is now open and can never again be closed.

He tells me about his older brother Christopher and how he died from a hunter's bullet back in the mid-1900s. I didn't even know he had a brother. I reach out a hand to comfort him, but he shakes his head and we return to silence.

We let the horses out one by one and clean out stalls, working in a comfortable cohesive manner. I begin to realize why Shaw has told me these things. He wants me to know I'm not alone, that he has lost someone too. I appreciate that so much. I want to tell him that, but from the looks we share I can tell he already knows.

More of the pack has come down to the barn only to realize a lot of the work is already done. We receive several lingering looks, but Shaw and I say nothing, ignoring it all and just focusing on our tasks. We keep silent even when we head up to breakfast together.

Shaw opens the screen door for me at the back of the house, but catches my arm to stop me from going inside. I look at him with a question in my eyes, but all he says is, "I'll see you after breakfast Lee," and then he's gone.

I wonder what that was about, but the kids calling from inside the house gets me moving and putting Shaw's actions towards the back of my mind for now, that is until several adult heads turn my way upon entering the kitchen. From their expectant looks I realize they think Shaw is right behind me, as if we're a pair now. Nope, is all I think as I wash my hands at the sink before grabbing a plate for breakfast.

"Is Shaw coming in for breakfast?" Martha asks over the children's chatter. The adults, I notice, are silent now as they wait for my answer.

"Umm, no Martha, he said he had things to do, but he'd see us later," I feel a light blush come over my cheeks, but I refuse to meet anyone's eyes.

"Oh I see, well perhaps we'll still save some food for him."

I just nod my head in response because I want this conversation to be over, fast. Is this why Shaw didn't come into the kitchen? Did he know they would be thinking we were together? Smart man if he did. I should probably thank him later for not coming to breakfast. I hold in a laugh as I think about all the women in the world who want a man to stick around for a meal and here I am thankful one didn't even show up, ha, this is awesome.

The smile I'm refusing to show fades a little as I realize I wouldn't mind sharing a breakfast with Shaw.

The smile in my eyes fades entirely as I wonder what that means. I guess it means that I see more substance in him now, he's not just a carefree playboy, there is real depth in him and I know our connection has deepened more. I feel comfortable with him, even safe. Yeah, I would enjoy breakfast with him.

I become suddenly aware of someone watching me and I look up to see Martha watching me intently, a small smile on her lips and a question in her eyes. I smile back placidly and finish eating breakfast.

I don't know how long I can take this mate-matchmaking crap and my thoughts turn more serious. Do they not understand we're just friends? That there isn't any love there? He's a good guy, but he's not my guy. I'm going through too much in my life to stop and think about love and settling down. Get real pack, get real and leave it alone.

~~~~~~

I spend most of my days around the pack house as it's the main pack property and is far enough away from regular humans to keep me out of trouble. "Yay me," I say to myself using sarcasm, but even with that sarcasm I knew it was for the best. Every hour that passes I seem to be getting worse, more on edge and more angry – deep breaths, deep breaths Lee, do not freak out. After a moment's pause I continue raking up the loose leaves in the backyard. How can there be leaves on the ground in August? I shake my head realizing just how much I've yet to learn and experience here in Montana. I've been given this task because we're going to be setting up for a birthday party out here in a couple of hours, should be fun. They are inviting several human families, so I've been warned to be on my best behavior. No pressure.

I pause in my actions – I freeze for just a brief moment in time. She's here again. Every time she shows up I can feel the hair on the back of my neck rise and the skin on my arms breaks out into goosebumps.

I can't see her, but I know she's here.

Is she behind me?

I spin around and there she is looking as innocent as the child she appears to be.

Is she really a child? Or is this some trick of her magic?

I try to uses my wolf senses to determine if this is all an illusion, but she looks real to me. Her pale blue t-shirt style dress reaches past her knees, and her white hair flows straight down to her slim waist. I notice she's placed a few more braids in her hair. Why? Does it mean something? She only had two small braids in her hair when she first appeared to me and now there appears to be at least ten. She's propped herself against the nearest tree and I notice the little werewitch is eyeing me with some amusement.

"Noticing some changes?" she asks me playfully, but I choose to ignore her question as it worries me that she can read me so well.

"What do you want little witch?" I say with a slight edge to my words, but in my focus on her I've missed something important.

Too late I realize we're not alone.

Chapter 5

I See You

LEE

"Who's that?" a soft voice asks behind me. A voice I know all too well and I spin around to see her.

"What's what Little Belle?" I ask the cute little girl in front of me hoping she isn't referring to who I think she is.

I hate having my back to the werewitch, but I don't want my behavior to frighten the little girl. Her name is Annabelle and she is the oldest of the Alpha's children, but I always call her Little Belle. Her hair is the same as her father's, very blonde. The long silken strands are braided back from her face and she's wearing a flower print shirt and blue shorts, a perfect outfit for this late summer day.

"Her," Annabelle answers simply as she points her arm towards something behind me. I feel a sense of dread as my eyes follow her movement, confirming, yes indeed she is pointing at the werewitch who is still standing next to the oak tree.

"Annabelle you can see her?" I whisper quietly, as shock stiffens up my muscles. I thought I was the only one who could see her. Is the werewitch finally showing herself to the pack? Or is this some sort of trick? Should I be more wary? Ugh! Why must she play games with me!?

"Of course I can I see her Lee, who is she?" the alpha's daughter asks me, so innocent and pure and I feel afraid for her as the witch flicks her intense blue eyes between us, and a small curling begins at the corner of her lips.

"She's a werewitch Little Belle, and I think she may want to do bad things. So birthday girl, I need you to go back inside," as I say this Little Belle tilts her head, looking the werewitch up and down completely nonplussed.

"A werewitch? But those aren't real. Daddy said they are just a myth meant to frighten children into being good."

"Well Little Belle, it appears they are real." I feel so afraid in this moment and yet her innocence can't help but bring a tender smile to my face.

"Aren't witches supposed to be ugly? She looks too pretty to be bad. And why is she so young? She can't be much older than me" she says as the werewitch takes a few steps toward us and I feel my hackles rise.

"Not all evil looks evil sweetheart," I tell her as I also step closer to the young wolf cub, my eyes never leaving the danger I see walking ever closer.

When the werewitch stretches out her arm to
Annabelle I quickly jump in front of her blocking her
from whatever the witch intended. "Go inside Little
Belle!" I growl out fiercely, too fiercely considering her
rank in the pack. However, in this moment I don't care
about her rank, I care about her safety and that is what
makes my tone so aggressive.

"But," Little Belle mumbles, but I cut her off
before she can continue.

"No Annabelle, go inside!" I say more firmly and
a few moments later I hear her quietly retreat back to the
safety of the house and some of the tension eases from
my shoulders. I am thankful she didn't put up a fight as
she felt the danger, I'm sure she did. Martha might be
out here soon as I didn't think to ask Little Belle not to
mention the werewitch. I'm not sure I would have asked
her to keep it a secret, but I can't think about that now,
its time to get rid of the witch.

"I could take her if I want to," came the eerie voice and goosebumps travel across my skin in a flash.

"Don't," it's the only word I say, but if I had to…I would fall to my knees and beg if that's what it took to protect that little girl. I am full of pride, but that child is innocent, so I would gladly do whatever the werewitch asked of me. That knowledge is something I never want the werewitch to know because I know without a doubt she would use it against me.

"I won't. I don't hurt children Lee. And in another time she and I could have been friends."

"Is that what you want? A friend?" I growl at her.

"Among other things, but it's too late for that now," she says solemnly, "I find it interesting though that you're so attached to her."

Fear trickles down my spine, but I refuse to let it show, "She's the alpha's daughter, surely you know that already."

"I do. I just wanted to see what your answer would be," and her smile looks a bit too smug with that last statement. She continues to circle me, but I never show her my back. I keep my eyes trained on her, not trusting her out of my line of vision, "What do you want witch? To kill another friend of mine?" I snarl after that last bit because I really do believe it was her. It must have been her – the dream felt too real for it not to be.

Her youthful face turns a little sad, "Yes, it was me Lee, I killed your friend."

I lunge for her before I can stop myself, but my arms never capture her as with a wave of her arm and a flash of blue power I am sent flying into the side of the shed with a hard thump.

"Now, now," she chides me, "No need for violence." Her tone reminds me of a teacher scolding a child on the playground…it makes me want to rip her throat out. I vaguely register how much of a monster that makes me – I want to kill what is essentially a child, but I push the thought away, I have no time for a conscience.

I huff in pain as I scramble back to my feet. Rage pounds through me and I want blood. "Why? Why would do it? Jeannie wasn't a threat to you! She and I were humans, we weren't meant to be werewolves! Why!? I have to know, I need it! Why?" My voice has grown louder and I'm sure any wolf listening can hear us, but I don't give a crap. I have to know why she would kill Jeannie and settle me with this cursed existence.

Her young face turns even sadder, but the pout on her lips doesn't soothe the need to kill and the wolf lunges forward inside me. I'm tempted, so tempted to free her; consequences be damned.

"It's not like I wanted to kill her, but I needed you to be a werewolf and I needed you to be here, not there. With Jeannie dead you had to stay, she was your last real connection to your home."

I growl at her feeling the wolf coming forward, but her smile stops me from setting the wolf completely free. "Aww come on now," she coaxes as if talking to a scared puppy, "Just let the wolf out, that's what we both want."

"Never!" I snarl desperately trying to push the wolf back down. She watches me intently as I struggle to calm down. I think she's enjoying it and I don't bother to hide the disgust from my face. A sliver of calm is all I hold onto as I ask, "Why do you need me?"

She looks almost happy as her lips curve upwards, "You already know the answer to that question." We stare at each other, assessing each other's moves and emotions – all the ways I could kill her roll through my mind, but I squash it down. Stay calm wolf, I tell the beast inside but her snarl tells me she's as ready to go as I am. Breathe, calm down, we need to know what she's planning. I feel the wolf calm down just a smidge, but she's not happy about it, not in the least. I'll have to deal with that later because right now a greater problem faces me.

"No I don't know! Why is it so important that I change? I'm nothing, a non-purebred, so why is it so important?" my voice has grown louder as my desperation has leeched to the surface. I hate that she can see the fear in me, but I need to know.

"Look into your heritage young one, and there will be the answers you seek," and with that she is gone.

My heritage? What the hell is so important about that? Her games and riddles are giving me a headache.

WEREWITCH

I fade away, making myself invisible to Lee. I wonder if she knows how often I watch her? I know she cannot feel me unless I allow her to, but does she realize how much I have learned about her these last few months? If not, she soon will. I leave Lee in a state of confusion. I giggle a little at the game I'm playing with her. It's been so long since I've had this much fun! I know it isn't quite fair and my sense of right and wrong eats at me a little, but I never have anyone to talk to or play with so this is nice.

"Remember the price, the end goal, you want this," I remind myself and the sense of doing wrong fades away. I need her, she's the key I've waited lifetimes for and I won't lose her now, I can't.

"Forgive me Nature," I beg to the silent woods around me as I now stand high up on a hill, far above the Centennial pack's home. I transported myself up here because I didn't want to walk all that way alone. Transporting is a useful skill, one among many I can do. I look toward the sky wondering if Nature is looking down upon me, "Forgive me," I call out to the blue sky above me, "But I can't live this way anymore! I was taken too young! Please understand. I took her presence here to mean you wished for me to have her. If I am wrong, please show me before it's too late. I don't want to take what you don't want to give…but I need her Nature, please let me have her."

I wait in the silence of the woods, waiting for an answer from Nature. I strain my ears to hear something, anything, yet all I hear is the chirping of birds and an occasional squirrel rustling through the leaves. Nothing responds and I sigh with the weight of the world upon me…I hope I'm not wrong. If I am wrong…I know Nature won't be forgiving.

~~~~~~

LEE

I'm sitting on one of the picnic benches in the backyard, facing the western side of the property, but my mind isn't on the surrounding beauty or the horses racing through the pasture, my mind is on what the werewitch said.

My heritage. My heritage, that's what she said. My heritage? I think with confusion as my right hand absently twirls the garden rake I'm supposed to be busy using. "What does she mean?" I wonder as my eyes stare off into nothing.

My heritage isn't a great mystery. I was adopted by an older couple when I was five. They couldn't have kids, so they decided to build a good home and adopt children to share it with. They were good people and if they had the money I think they would have adopted more children. My Mom was a wonderful lady and in her early fifties when I came to live with them and my Dad was a kind, quiet soul nearing his sixties, like I said they were older. They died in a car accident when I was still in college. It was traumatic for me, but I also know that's the way they would have wanted to go...together.

I shake my head, no the witch definitely couldn't be talking about them. They were sweet and kind and good, they wouldn't be mixed in with all this crap. No, she was talking about the time before I was adopted, the true great mystery of my life: my birth parents.

What is there to say about my birth parents? Admittedly, not much as it was a closed adoption. They didn't want me to know them, and they didn't want to know me. Enough said. At least that's what I thought up until about fifteen minutes ago.

Now though? Well, now I find myself wondering who they were, what they were, and if they knew about things like werewolves and werewitches. Are they related to this werewitch? Did they do her wrong? Did they make her a deal? What is this Rumpelstiltskin? Get real, they made no deal.   A sigh escapes me as the futility of the situation overcomes me. I don't have any real resources to find my birth parents and they seem to be the key as to what is going on. I can't ask any of the cops in the pack to look up any of this information…can I? There might just be a way after all, hmmm.

I know sitting here wondering about what I may never know won't do me any good, but it's hard to just shake it off and let it go, especially when there's a werewitch hanging about and threatening children. What's next? Will she kill somebody? I don't know and that's what worries me.

Eventually I stand up and get back to work. The pack won't be happy to come out here and find I haven't finished raking the yard. As I grab the rake it suddenly dawns on me that Annabelle never came back outside, and neither did any of the adult wolves…what is going on? I quickly rake the rest of the yard as fast as I can and gather up the leaves into bags. I take a quick look around and nod my head, saying to myself, "Okay looks good, they can start setting up for the party now."

"Yes we can," says the young wolf Kaley from the back porch.

"I got distracted for a little bit," I say, trying to feel out if I'm in trouble or something.

"Yeah so Annabelle said. You told her quite a werewitch story. Where would someone like you hear about werewitches anyway?" Kaley asks in a tone of slight accusation.

Kaley has short coppery colored hair and honey brown eyes. She seems friendly enough, but she definitely has the attitude of a teenager most of the time. Most I know about her is she's really impatient for her first wolf change to happen.

Damn, damn, double damn. On one hand they believe I told Annabelle some fairy story, on the other they're wondering where I learned such details about werewitches in the first place and I honestly feel bad that they don't believe Annabelle.

"Oh around, some of the pack has shared a few tales with me," I reply in a nonchalant manner, not wanting to raise her suspicions.

"Huh," is all Kaley says as she slides a few boxes of decorations and other supplies outside the door. "Come and grab some of these please."

"Sure," I say as I quickly put the rake back in the shed. "What makes you think it was just a story anyway?" I ask and then silently curse myself for bringing it back up. Stupid curiosity.

Kaley shrugs her young shoulders in an offhanded manner, "Because werewitches aren't real and if they were…then you guys wouldn't have lived to tell the tale."

I laugh because I know that's the response she's looking for, "Oh really?"

"Really," she affirms as she looks through boxes. Ha, if they only knew.

Several other packmates come out of the house and for the next few hours we get busy turning the backyard into an awesome looking birthday bash for

Little Belle. There are balloons, streamers, picnic tables with colorful tablecloths, and several games set up for all the children.

"You guys really do go all out for a kid's birthday," I say with more than a touch of admiration.

"Heck yes we do!" shouts Maggie and I'm a little surprised to see the level of her excitement, which must show on my face because she immediately defends herself, "What? Birthdays are fun."

"Yeah, no, I'm not disagreeing with you, just didn't realize you liked them so much."

"Well I do, so there. If you got a problem with it Lee, I could always take you on in another round of combatives?"

"Yeah let's not do that Maggie," I say through my laughter before heading inside to get ready for the party which starts at four this afternoon.

Chapter 6

Some Birthdays Are Bad

LEE

Today is Little Belle's tenth birthday, and she's been talking about this day for weeks. She is the oldest cub of our alphas and she is a delight to be around. She's always filled with so much happiness that you can't help but be happy when you're around her. I'm not the only one who feels this way, it's the whole pack. Annabelle just has that spark inside her that makes others feel better. I find I actually like all the pack children, or cubs as they are more commonly called when we're not around humans. I didn't think I would, but I do. The cubs are great; they bring the adults back down to earth and they make us all realize it's the simple things in life that are important.

I think about how happy all the children will be when they see this awesome backyard. I'm helping set up the last of the games before all the kids get here. Though she may be a werewolf, Little Belle and all the other cubs go to a normal human school. So naturally all the cubs have lots of human children for friends. I shrug my shoulders thinking it's not really a big deal, course if I were one of the human parents and found out my little Sally or Joe was having a playdate with something that could kill, well I wouldn't be thrilled. I shake my head and continue to help with setup.

I look around the backyard taking stock of what we've managed to accomplish in the last few hours. Streamers are everywhere draping from tree to tree, Maggie and another wolf I don't remember the name of, maybe Emily? Well Maggie and what's her face are tying balloons to the picnic tables and some of the small bushes. It looks like a kid's birthday paradise. I'm almost jealous.

My nose catches the scent of all the good things being cooked in the kitchen every time the door on the back porch opens. My stomach rumbles a little at the thought of putting a tasty pulled pork sandwich in my mouth...mmmm. I close my eyes as I breathe it in more. It's going to be so yummy.

"Hey Fluffy! Stop drooling!" a deep voice calls out across the backyard. My shoulders tense up of their own accord as I turn to face that well-known voice.

"Shut up fur ball!" I respond with a smile on my lips.

Shaw is grinning at my response and he hops over the back gate and jogs on over to where I'm now stacking hay bales around the campfire pit. He has a natural grace about him and it's obvious in every movement that he's comfortable in his own skin. I envy him that. I envy all of the other werewolves that because

I don't feel comfortable in my own skin. I'm embracing as much of the wolf as I can, but without changing she and I are not one and I feel so awkward and jerky most of the times.

"Need some help good looking?" Shaw asks in his typical playful manner. The serious guy from the barn is gone. Is it all a façade? I don't know.

"Stop flirting and help me stack the hay goofball," upon seeing his lack of movement and raised brow I narrow my eyes into slits and add, "Please?"

"Of course I'll help you Lee, especially since the guests are arriving out front. And if I was flirting with you, you'd know it sugar lips," he says with a wink. I do my best not to smile at his playful statement, but I'm learning it's hard to stay angry or unhappy with Shaw around. He's not a jerk, even if we got off to a rough start initially. I now know he's a decent guy and I find myself liking him more and more. I'm glad he's in my pack.

I stop thinking about Shaw as werewolves and humans, both adult and children, start filling up the backyard. It's gonna be a heck of an afternoon. This is the close the pack has let me to this many humans since I came here in June, and I want to show them they can trust me not to freak out.

So a birthday party with humans? No big deal, let's do this.

WEREWITCH

I want to go to the birthday party. I want to eat cake and play games with the children, but I can't. Not only do people tend to freak out when they see me, but since I have lived for a millennia I'm not really a child anymore. I wouldn't fit in with all those innocent children I see laughing and smiling in the backyard. Besides most werewolves get a bit twitchy around me anyway. Not sure why exactly, maybe it's the magic?

Either way I've learned it's best to be alone, no matter how lonely that life may get.

I lean against the big oak tree in the pack's backyard, knowing none of them can see me or sense my presence. As I look around at all the happy faces I find myself in envy of these children who know nothing about the evils in this world.

Hmm, some would say I am one of those evils I muse to myself. I know Lee would say it because of what happened to Jeannie. I glance over at my precious Lee, the one who I need more than air to breathe. She seems to be doing well, perhaps too well?

I narrow my eyes as I look her over, her black hair is loose about her shoulders and she's dressed casual in her pale blue V-neck shirt and white jean shorts. Not exactly the most party-orientated outfit I've ever seen, but she still looks nice. I continue to watch her for the next several minutes and I find myself wondering why she never wears any dresses? Does she not like them? She doesn't seem all that girly, but she must want to be girly once in a while. Doesn't she want to look pretty for Shaw? I've noticed the looks between them and it adds to my guilt, a guilt I have to push away constantly. He could be her mate and after all I have lost in my own life I don't want to separate her from all the possibilities that were stolen from me so long ago.

"Guide me Nature," I whisper softly even though I know none of the partygoers can hear me. Every day I watch Lee I feel more connected to her and my indecision intensifies. I shouldn't have come to her so early and she would have changed a dozen times over by now. It was my folly that led us to this.

I turn my mind back to lighter thoughts and I wonder what Lee would think of the women from my original time?

A smile quickly spreads across my face as I realize Lee would probably have fit in quite well as a Viking. She is stubborn and proud, plus she picks up on fighting techniques quickly. Yes, she would have been a heck of a Viking. Back then women always wore some style of dress, even when there was a battle going on. A dress was always worn. A great many women wore breeches as well, but always with a short dress.

Would my mother be shocked by how much skin is shown by the women of today? Maybe? Or maybe not, as witches always do seem to be more open to the changes occurring in the world.

A tender smile crosses my lips at the thought of my mother before looking down at myself. A preteen girl, not fully developed is what I see. A flower print dress covers my young body, draping all the way down to my mid-calf. I'm wearing white sandals that almost match my long white hair. My hair wasn't always this color that came with being a werewitch. I've pulled my hair into a low side ponytail and it hangs over my left shoulder. The multiple braids within my mass of hair are from a time when women wore braids not just for beauty but to show strength and courage. I pick one up and toy with it gently. I stare at the blue glass bead tied at the end with a leather strip. This one is special, this is one my mother first braided and she gave me the bead on my tenth birthday.

Little Annabelle wouldn't even understand the importance of something so small I scoff as I look at the tables holding her many presents. Children are so spoiled I think with a shake of my head. They know nothing of sacrifice, hardship, and loss...terrible terrible loss.

Annabelle looks abundantly happy, completely untouched by darkness as all children should be. I envy all the cubs that. I know why she is so special and soon so will Lee, but for now she is simply a happy wolf child.

I find myself tiring of waiting on Lee and as my eyes catch sight of a group of young girls playing near a rose bush, I decide it's time to give Lee a little push.

LEE

The birthday party is in full swing now and its going well. I'm doing great, the beast inside is feeling calm. We are not going to mess up this birthday party. I smile as I fill up several more cups with punch juice for the kids when I hear a child cry, "Ow!"

I look over, as do several parents and all of the wolves; we take stock of the situation. One of the human children, a young girl has scratched her hand on one of the many rosebushes that line the sides of the house. Shelby and her human friend Karen, both nurses, go over to the girl to check if she's ok. I know I'm not needed for this situation, but that's when it hits me like a ton of bricks.

Her blood, I smell her blood and it's a sweet scent. I begin to feel hypnotized by the *thump, thump, thump* of her little heartbeat. My hand is still clasped around a plastic cup of punch, but my eyes have narrowed in on my target and nothing else matters. My tongue licks along my teeth feeling each tooth shift and grow sharper and sharper with every passing second.

I take one step forward to bring myself closer to my prey when a clear strong voice breaks through my mind's haze. I know that voice and I recognize the authority in it. It is my female Alpha's voice I hear, sharp and strong it reaches my ears. Her voice is too quiet for the humans to hear, but I hear it easily from my position across the yard from her, "Stop. Lee stop, stand still and close your eyes." I don't even resist her command as I realize how close I am to killing that girl in this crowded backyard full of wolves and humans. Damn this is going to go over real well. I keep my eyes closed and try to breath steady, but still my ears train themselves on the heartbeat of that little girl and my nose continues to twitch as the scent of blood fills my nostrils. Oh damn, it is so tempting, I just want a taste. I feel the wolf coming forward and I know I don't have much time before all hell will break loose.

SHAW

I heard Martha's softly spoken command and my eyes zoomed in on Lee. I could see she was shaking and trying desperately to hold it together. I could smell the aggression and the eagerness coming off her in silent waves and I knew my whole pack was immediately on alert. We never knew when Lee might snap and that little girl's blood had obviously become the tipping point.

I hear my alpha whisper as children continue to play and the humans laugh and enjoy their beers, totally unaware of the danger. "Shaw," Gregory whispers to me, "Take Lee and get her out of here. Now." I bow my head slightly in his direction acknowledging the command and try to casually meander my way across the backyard.

I am almost to Lee's side when I hear her soft whimper, I stifle a curse as I pick up my pace knowing we only have seconds before things turn into a bloodbath. I wrap my arm around her shoulders and turn her towards the house. She is stiff in my arms and I can feel her body trembling as she tries to control her wolf. Quickly I push her along, getting her around the house and to my truck. I pull open the door not wanting to waste any time. "Get in," I say quietly next to Lee's ear. Her smell is running over me and I can sense her struggle is at an all-time high. I slam the door after she hops into the seat, but not before I notice her hands have turned into paws. "Shit," I say under my breath, not even checking to see if the human kids are around. I get into the driver's seat as fast as possible, start the truck and we take off down the drive kicking up a little dust as we go. I spare a quick glance at Lee to see black hair has started growing out of her arms and her face has begun to change. Damn, I do not want her to wolf out on me while we're still in the truck. Think, think! I gotta get her to calm down stat.

"So Lee, how would you like to go for a run with me?" I'm doing my best to keep my tone calm and steady, but my inner wolf has picked up on her agitated state and I can feel him wanting to come out. I stamp down the urge to change and focus on bringing Lee back from the brink. "What do you say Lee, wanna go into the woods and have some fun?" I try to put a little lightness in my tone, but inside I'm freaking out. There's no manual for this. C'mon Lee keep it together gal.

She turns her head to look at me and as I glance her way I see the wolf in her eyes. No longer are her eyes the warm brown I've gotten so used to, nope now they are a luminescent blue showing me the predator within. I won't lie, seeing her wolfish side brings out a surge of desire because a female wolf is still a female wolf and those eyes are doing something to me that I don't want to dwell on for too long. I breathe in deep to calm myself and wait for her response. She looks confused as she thinks over my question, but it helps. Her change has slowed down and now the hair on her arms is receding and her face is looking a little more human.

"Just a walk in the woods?" she asks, but it comes out deep as her voice rumbles with a wolfish sound.

"Yep, just a walk. You and me, no one else keeping tabs on you. It'll be a nice little getaway, yeah?"

Her face is almost back to normal and she breathes in and out slowly. I glance over again and see her brown eyes are looking back at me.

"Okay," she says softly nodding her head. I reach over and grab her hand. "You're ok Lee, it's going to be alright." Her eyes glance from our joined hands to my face and she nods again. We remain silent for a while as I continue to drive us further away from civilization.

"That was close Shaw, too close," she says breaking the silence we've been riding in.

I squeeze her hand, "Yeah, yeah it was." I don't want to start our ongoing argument of her changing – she's just gotten herself back under her control.

"I wanted to kill that little girl."

"Let's not think about that right now, let's just enjoy the ride." I roll her window down letting the wind in and I watch as a peace settles over her features. I feel a calmness come over me too, but it doesn't last long.

"Where are we?" Lee asks me as I pull off the gravel road and onto a dirt path. I pulled off the main road about 15 minutes ago and now we're completely surrounded by woods. The afternoon sun has slipped further down turning the day into evening.

"We're up in the mountains on the back side of the pack property," I inform her as I bring the truck to a stop. Neither one of us gets out as she looks around; getting used to the new smells.   "Why   not   just drive through the pastures to get here then?" I remain silent for a moment and Lee turns her gaze onto me. "Mostly because we would have had to walk farther that way as the road doesn't lead all the way up here, and because the people at the party would have noticed a truck driving through an open pasture." She frowns, but says nothing. I can sense her struggle…I can sense it all the time and I want to help her. I don't know why she's so afraid of being a wolf. Does she despise us? A flash of rage goes through me at the thought, but then I remember what Gregory told us when Lee first came to the pack about how she was attacked and the woman who died that night. I remember Lee only talking about her friend, Jeannie was her name, very little. Maybe I would hate our kind too if that had happened to me. I know I hated humans for a while after my brother's death. Maybe she just needs to see we're not the monsters of her nightmares.

"Well are we going for a walk or what?" Lee's question breaks me away from my thoughts. "Yep," I say opening the door and stepping outside. I breathe in deep enjoying the smells up here. It always has felt like home to me with the cool wind blowing through the trees, and the scent of animals all around here. Up here I feel free, I feel wild and I love it.

"Ready to turn?" I ask casually as Lee walks around to my side of the truck. My question causes her to freeze in place and I see a wash of panic cross her face. I don't like seeing her that way, I prefer it when she stands up for herself. I like seeing her strength. This fear she has bothers the hell out of me. She's my friend, I know it's a crazy friendship and half the pack doesn't understand how it even came to be, but she's my friend and I want to help her.

"No Shaw," she says firmly, taking a step away from me.

"Lee," I start, but she's having none of it and walks a few more steps away shaking her head furiously. Her near jet black hair swishes from side to side before settling again just below her shoulders. Gosh she's got beautiful hair and I can't help but wonder what her wolf would look like. Will her hair be black like that when she's in her wolf form? I remember her arms from earlier and realize yes, yes her wolf would be dark. The image of a black wolf with intense blue eyes rolls through my mind and my inner wolf lets out a yip at the mental picture. I shake my head, directing myself to re-focus on the present.

"Lee, it's just us. You're safe here."

I need her to believe she's safe with me because it actually hurts to think she wouldn't trust me. I mean sure we didn't get off on the right foot, what with me kissing her and her clawing my face, but I think we've moved past that. I need her to believe I would never do her any harm, but as she spins around I can see the set of her jaw and I know it's going to be a fight.

"Am I?" she asks coolly, raising one of those dark finely arched brows at me. I feel another shaft of desire, but again I ignore it because she is not just another female, she is my friend and I won't ruin it for a roll in the hay I'm not even supposed to have with a wolf I don't want as a mate.

I'm thrown off by not only the defiance I see in her stance and eyes, but also by my own reaction to it, "Are you what?" I ask taking a few steps towards her.

"Am I safe here?" she asks quietly, some of her anger fading away as I see her scanning my face. Is she looking for some sign of a trick? I wouldn't do that. I may be a bit of a jokester, but I wouldn't do that to her, especially not now, not when I might actually be making progress in getting her to shift.

"Yes you are," I say firmly stepping even closer to her. She's now within reach, which is good in case she takes off running. I wait to see what she will do. Her eyes keep jumping all over the place and it takes me a moment to realize she's looking for something, she's searching for something in the shadows of the woods and I wonder what she sees. My wolf ears are straining and besides the occasional bird or squirrel we are alone up here.

"There's no one here, except for you and me. We're alone Lee," I say raising my hand to touch her face; I'm trying to reassure her as I sense her agitation rising again. Suddenly she closes her eyes and tilts her head slightly to the left. I swear it's like she can hear someone talking in her ear and then I see her body shiver. She opens her eyes and the wolf is there, "No," she croaks out with some fear in her voice, "No we're not."

"Lee, it's ok. You can trust me to help you change."

"No," she says again more forcefully and as her eyes connect with mine I feel a tingle run down my spine and the hairs on the back of my neck start to rise. "No, but I do need your help keeping the wolf under control."

I sigh realizing she's probably not going to change tonight, "If that's really what you want Lee, ok. What do you need-" before the final words leave my mouth her hands have grabbed the front of my jacket and then her mouth is slamming into mine. My mind totally blanks as I feel the desperation in her kiss and the desire I've been pushing down for her for months comes roaring full force to the surface. I try to find some control as she slides my jacket off. "Lee, are you sure?" I ask as her hands slip under my shirt.

My wolf growls inside me, upset that I'm trying to stop this moment from happening, but I ignore him. I tilt her head up so she has to look at me, "Lee?" I ask again scanning her face. "Yes," she whispers and that's all I need. I should be a better man and stop, but I'm just not that guy. My wolf has grown excited as I peel off her shirt and jean shorts and we resume kissing like our lives depend upon it. Without even thinking about it I've backed her up to a tree and I've picked her up so her toned legs can wrap around my naked waist. Damn, I'm going to be in so much trouble when we get back home.

Chapter 7

All the Pieces Fall

LEE

My nails sharpened into the claws I was now becoming used to and I dragged them along Shaw's muscular back, cutting deep and leaving red gouges from his shoulders to his lower back. Not scratches, gouges and my wolf approves of my actions. I can feel the blood trickle over my hands and my excitement grows even more. I hear Shaw growl as our frenzied lovemaking continues.

I've had to keep the wolf at bay for so long, but the smell of that girl's blood unleashed something inside, something I was slightly afraid of. I didn't want to feel that darkness, so now here I was, practically stripped naked making out with Shaw and he was definitely helping to satisfy urges I thought were long since dormant. I thought I really could change with Shaw, but when the werewitch giggled in my ear, that possibility was destroyed and I snapped. I did the first thing that came to mind to appease the wolf's desire to be free – I kissed Shaw.

I could feel my inner wolf rise closer to the surface and I found I couldn't resist her completely. My wolf wants out and as I feel the rising desperation within I try again to appease her so I won't shift completely. So with my lengthening canines I open my jaws wide and bit down hard onto Shaw's muscled left shoulder. My wolf whimpers with the pleasure of the bite and the taste of blood trickling down our throat. I feel Shaw freeze for a brief moment before throwing his head back to let out a long howl – making my wolf quiver with even more excitement. I was getting lost in the moment and was completely unprepared for when Shaw bit me back in return. His teeth were sunk deep into my left shoulder and I could feel the blood trickle down my collarbone and breast as me and the wolf whimpered together this time. My wolf and I had never been so in tune and with Shaw satisfying both of us it was a heady feeling. I bite down harder on his shoulder trying to keep the wolf inside and he once again returns the favor. Our teeth are sunk deep and it feels glorious.

Biting…that's what mates do, but I knew Shaw would understand the reason behind the bite, for it was not tender it was frantic and harsh. And in this moment I didn't care about the rules, I needed him and I would deal with the consequences later.

The pain of the bite grounds me to the present, but just barely as more pleasure runs through my body and I let loose a loud growl. Shaw speeds up the pace and I can't think anymore as his hips slam into mine. We share one more bloody kiss as the smell of sweat, blood, and desire flood the evening air and are intoxicating to my wolf. I let out another growl as I lose myself in Shaw, just as he seems to be losing himself in me. More growls, snaps, and snarls fill the air as the minutes go by and we become completely absorbed in each other.

A short time later after satisfying the frenzy, we were spent. Neither of us said anything as we panted, trying to catch our breath. Shaw slid me back down to my feet and leaned his forehead against mine. His wolf's golden eyes fade back to the more human midnight blue – such a mesmerizing blue. One of his hands still rests on my hip, the other is resting against the tree trunk above my head. I notice we are both still out of breath, but I also can feel my wolf's senses are at an all-time high and it feels amazing. How had I gone this long without feeling like this? Everything felt so heightened and yet somehow I felt a bit more under control than I had since first getting bitten.

"Your eyes are still the wolf Lee," Shaw says calmly as his breathing slows down and I freeze in place, but he continues, "Breathe, relax, you're in control."

Instead of shoving him away and putting up my defenses I decide to take his advice. I breathe deep, closing my eyes as I do so. I find myself surprised and yet flattered to hear him tell me I'm in control instead of telling me to change. Is this another sign of the friendship we've developed over the last few months? I think so and I bite back the smile I can feel forming. I breathe deeply again and his mountain scent fills my nostrils.

Suddenly it hits me…what have I done?

I just slept with my friend Shaw…did I just ruin a friendship over something so stupid? Over sex? My wolf disagrees, and I think it's because she wants to be mated to Shaw and his wolf. Why, why did I have to bite him? Crap, another problem to deal with.

As I continue to breathe nice and steady I feel my wounds healing and my senses pick up Shaw's healing process as well. I still can't get enough of that fast-healing process.

"So," Shaw says into the quiet of the night, "Are we mates now?" I snap my eyes open and grumble out one word, "Crap." Shaw takes a step back as I search for my shorts.

"Hey, you were the one to bite me honey," Shaw tosses the words at me and I visibly cringe as I manage to get my legs in my shorts. "I know," I say as Shaw pulls on his pants and then his boots. I scan his face and he looks, well neither happy nor angry, "I know Shaw, but you know why I did it."

"Yeah," he says matter-of-factly, "To appease your inner wolf so you wouldn't change. But Lee," He continues in an exasperated tone as he zips up his jeans and I begin to realize just how pissed off he is, "How long do you honestly think that will work for?"

I debate on what to say as we continue to dress, and I end up settling on playing dumb, "Are you suggesting we make this a common occurrence Shaw?" I even try to put a flirty smile with it, but I've never been that girl so it's an uncomfortable feeling.

He straight up growls at me as he pulls on his shirt, not bothering to wipe the blood off from his back, "Stop, don't even try to joke around about this Lee, this is serious."

I bow my head feeling ashamed because he's right. "I know, I know it would have been bad if it were a human Shaw." Shaw straightens his clothes and runs his fingers through his hair before he looks at me and there's a darkness brewing in his eyes, "Listen Lee, a human male wouldn't have survived what you did to me." I feel the tension ripple between us as I think about what I did to Shaw – the bloody gouges on his back and the deep bite in his shoulder. If he were human, that blood loss would have led to death out here in the woods. Thinking about it repulses and excites me at the same time and Shaw can tell because I see his mouth thin into a stern white line. Is he disgusted? His next words seem to confirm that, "Change Lee. Change. If you don't it will only get worse." I open my mouth to respond, but he puts his hand up to cut off any response I would have made.

He takes what appears to be a calming breath before he speaks again, "You'll lose control someday and what happens if no one is there to save you? You could hurt one of the kids, human or wolf it doesn't matter. If you snap you'll kill." I let his words sink in and the uneasiness I have been feeling for months doubles making me feel sick.

"I can't," is all I manage to tell him. I know he's picking up on my distress because I see a change come over his face. He's trying to find out what I won't share.

"Why not?" he demands quietly as we both get back in the truck, our run for the night is a ridiculous idea now. I remain silent as he steers us along the dirt path to the main road. I can feel him glancing at me, still waiting for an answer. I continue to remain silent for another ten minutes before I give him the only answer I can, the truth, "Because she wants me to," I whisper into the dark cab.

~~~~~~

LEE

The pack has gathered inside the Alpha's house. Some are sitting on the multiple couches and some are standing, but all are gathered in the living room. There is a loud silence as I finish recapping all about the werewitch and what she has told me over the last few months. I see the faces of my pack, and stunned is the only word that seems to work in this situation.

I told them about the first time she came to me and how I thought it was a hallucination after the attack, I told them about the things she told me and how she wants me to change into a wolf more than anything. I tell them about how I asked them questions about werewitches and Maggie said to never do what they tell you to do. As I share all this, I find myself feeling so tired and so drained - did all of this really start only three months ago? It feels like so much longer than that, and yet I feel relieved…I am so relieved that I don't have to keep this secret any longer.

Finally the silence is broken by Petroff, Gregory's younger cousin. He stands up saying what I imagine most of them are thinking, "She's lying." He looks around as no one says a word, "She's got to be lying, this can't be true. Werewitches aren't real. They are a myth!" His voice has risen at this point and I can feel how charged the air is.

"She's not lying," Gregory calmly states and no one in the room argues with him. Still I see the confusion, the curiosity, the fear, and yes even the anger as they realize how much I've been hiding. They realize now why I've acted so strangely, but it still doesn't sit well with them.

Kaley is the one to speak next, "Should Lee leave?" Several surprised faces greet this question, but mine isn't one of them. At the offended looks Kaley quickly elaborates, "I mean is it safe for the rest of the pack for her to be here when there is a werewitch hanging around her like a, well like a grim reaper?"

I can see several of them thinking it over, and I say nothing in my defense because this, this is their decision to make and I had betrayed them by not telling them the truth from the beginning. I had lost my right to vote on this and it suddenly hit me how much that stung. Ugh. It seems like I was destined to do it all wrong no matter what I did.

"She is pack," Martha states quietly, but firmly, "Her trouble is our trouble, until the Alpha says otherwise." I feel comforted by Martha's decree, but I also feel unworthy of it.

We all wait until Gregory nods his affirmative, which is then followed by nods from the other males and females of the pack. Though they nod, we can all feel the tension in the room and it is draining and exhausting and I can't cope with much more of this. I'm destroying so much, and I can't help but feel worse and worse with each passing moment.

I find myself standing alone in my own corner, an outsider always. Shaw has not said a word, but I do not expect his support for I used him to stave off the wolf in order to defy a werewitch. An action that may very well have put him in extreme danger, and an action that has definitely put our friendship on the rocks.

Ugh, damn! What was I thinking?

Oh that's right, I rail at myself, I was thinking I didn't want to turn into a wolf, so I used a packmate to quench that urge. I used somebody in a sexual way, I feel self-disgust roll over me and I can't even look Shaw's way. I refuse to look him in the eye. I've lost respect for myself and I no longer deserve his. I'm not this person I admonish myself again and again. As a human I didn't sleep around, why oh why couldn't I just give in and change?

That's it, I think to myself, it's time to change, time to let the werewitch have what she wants because fighting her is ruining what's left of my life. My wolf wants to change, but I feel her resistance now as she doesn't want the werewitch to win, man she is stubborn.

Most of the pack has filed out of the room by now. Some have moved into the kitchen, and others have gone outside – no doubt to talk about all this and come to some kind of decision.   Bill and another cop in our pack called Marvin left to head to the station. They're hoping they can look up more about my birth parents, which may help us figure out that weird clue the werewitch gave us about my heritage being the key. They said the police database may have answers. I don't plan on getting my hopes up. Shelby and Peggy also went into town, they want to scour the books at the library for any information about werewitches…great. I mean, c'mon any of the information they find is going to be in the fiction section and there's no way to know if any of it is accurate.

To my surprise, Shaw has hung around. He's leaning up against the open entryway to the living room, but I continue to keep my eyes off him, so I have no idea what emotions are crossing his face.

I notice Martha speaking urgently with Gregory and a name catches my attention as she looks my way several times. *Emmaline.*

Who's Emmaline? I wonder when suddenly Martha calls out, "Lee, come with me."

There is no please in that command, and a command is what that is. I immediately step forward closing the distance between us. I find myself thankful for the reprieve I'll get by being out of sight of Shaw.

"I need to speak with you in the kitchen," Martha continues as she turns that way. I nod as I follow her down the hallway, but my wolf's ears pick up on Gregory saying, "We need to talk Shaw."

Crap. I physically cringe, and am thankful that Martha isn't looking at me.

They know.

Those are the only two words bouncing around in my brain as I continue to follow her into the now empty kitchen. Sometimes heightened wolf senses are a curse around here.

Martha has barely allowed me to sit down before she addresses the topic I'm dreading beyond belief.

"So, you and Shaw," she pauses as if waiting for me to fill in the blanks, but I refuse to give her anything. "What's going on there exactly?" I glance up quickly seeing too much intellect in her hazel eyes and I drop my eyes back to the table.

"Nothing," I say as blandly as possible. Hoping against hope she just lets it go.

"Nothing?" she questions as her right brow arches upward. Dang, here it comes.

"Have you two mated?" Before I can help myself, I cringe, which causes her to narrow her eyes. I know honesty is the only way to go, but I hate sharing this information. This was supposed to be private, just between Shaw and I, and that's lasted all of a few hours.

"Umm…not, not mated exactly Martha."

"Then what exactly?" I'm so embarrassed I can feel my face flushing a deep red. This isn't going to be pretty.

"Umm, well," I find myself hesitating, trying to find the right words, "We were together recently, but we're not bound to each other."

"Why?" That's all she asks, just one word.

"Why what?"

"Why were you together?" she growls lowly.

Man, gotta respect Martha, she doesn't hold back one bit. I take a deep breath before spilling my guts. I don't want to, but alphas are compelling and can tell when you lie.

"So my wolf wouldn't emerge." I finish my story, with my eyes looking down at the table. I don't want to see the look in Martha's eyes. I can already feel the anger rolling off of her and I cannot face it.

My confession is followed by a long silence and not the pleasant kind. My shoulder muscles are bunching from the tension. My head is down, my eyes lowered, and my hands are clenched together in my lap.

The next time Martha speaks, her voice is laced with so much anger and I know her wolf is close to the surface, "Are you telling me Lee, that you used one of your packmates to blow off some steam in order to prevent the most natural thing of our kind?"

"Yes," I say humbly just wanting to curl up and hide from her eyes. "But the werewitch-" I don't get to finish that statement as Martha jumps in.

"Why not a human? They are just play things anyway. So why not use one of them to blow off steam?" her voice is dripping with sarcasm, and she continues in a tidal wave of emotion I have never seen from her. "Why Shaw? Of all the werewolves in this pack, wait, no, what am I saying? You should never use another wolf for sex, especially to prevent the change. Never Lee. Mating is sacred amongst our kind, you know this and yet you bit him. I have told you all of the rules before."

She doesn't say it, but I feel her disappointment and another piece inside me seems to chip away. I've done this all wrong and now I've let down another person I respect.

"I know," I say quietly as my head hangs lower in renewed shame, "I know. I was afraid of what the werewitch wanted. Plus," I add quickly as I see a fierce expression cross Martha's face, "It was lucky it was Shaw and not a human."

That grabs Martha's attention as I knew it would, but I don't have a moment to relax as she questions me sharply, "Why? What happened?" This of course leads me to explain in more detail what happened out in the woods earlier. Is there no end to my shame? I know the whole pack will know about Shaw and I within an hour, two at the most. Why couldn't that part of our lives have stayed even a little bit private? I can't believe I had sex with Shaw only a few hours ago…feels like a lifetime ago now and I feel like I've aged ten years since those frenzied moments. I shake my head refusing to think about how right my teeth felt in his shoulder and how his howl made me shiver, nope, not going to think about it at all right now.

Martha actually looks shocked after I'm done telling her what happened with Shaw and I in the woods. I gloss over some of it because I find myself not wanting to share everything, I actually want to keep some of it to myself. Her mouth opens and closes several times before she regains some of her composure. Finally she speaks, "Gregory and I were going to have Shaw be your bodyguard to help fight off the werewitch and the change as you seem to listen so well to his advice, but after this," she shakes her head before continuing, "The female packmates will rotate shifts, myself included. Two females will be assigned to you at all times, and none of the males will be allowed around you if you're alone for some reason. Got it?"

Her last statement has me blushing again because she makes it sound like I can't control myself, but who am I to be upset?

For all I know she may be right, I may not be able to control myself at all anymore.

Did I find it all a little extreme? Duh, but I didn't want a repeat with Shaw, well at least not much of a repeat.

Wait, did I just think that?

Did I really want to be with Shaw again?

My inner wolf quivered slightly and I froze, oh no…no no no. I don't want a mate and I know for sure he doesn't either. Maybe Martha was right, maybe this was the best way to keep us all safe.

"Who's Emmaline?" I ask instead hoping to get Martha off the subject of Shaw. She remains quiet for several seconds before answering, "She's a local witch-"

"What!?" I don't even bother to hide my shock as I cut her off.

"If you'd let me finish," Martha says with a glare that has me shutting my lips together tight, "As I was saying, Emmaline is a town witch. She has helped us out once or twice before. She's a kind witch, nothing like your werewitch and I thought maybe she could help us. Of course she may just turn and run as I have no idea if she has enough magic to help us against a werewitch."

I don't say anything until Martha asks, "Well?"

I gulp before answering, "Well…a witch? Seriously? Does the whole pack know about her? Can we trust her to be on our side?"

"She's not a wolf so I wouldn't trust her a hundred percent if I were you, but yes I'm sure she'll be on our side because a werewitch would be competition for her and witches don't like that."

"Geez, I learn something new every day around you people," I say with a soft laugh.

"Hmmph, imagine how much you would learn if you only embraced being a wolf fully."

Hmm, great, good to know that peace lasted all of about five minutes.

~~~~~~~~~~~~~~~~~~~~~~~~~~~~~~~~~~

SHAW

While Lee shared her story with the pack I did my best to blend into the background. Lee and I had taken quick showers, separately of course, after coming back to the house, since several of the humans were still hanging around I thought it best to keep Lee away from them until they had all headed out.

Poor Lee, I can tell she hasn't realized that the whole damn pack knows what we've been up to. After we got back I insisted we get cleaned up. I told her it was to help her relax more before addressing the pack, but really I was hoping to wipe out some of the smell. Even after our showers though her scent is still on me and mine lingers on her, I can smell it from across the room; courtesy of those damn bites. I'm frustrated, but my wolf approves of my scent on her. *Mate*, he growls in my head, but I ignore him. Damn, I shouldn't have given into that urge, but once her teeth had broken the skin on my shoulder, my reaction was instinctive to mark her in return, course I wanted to punish her a little bit too for using me as an outlet in the first place.

She's been keeping her eyes trained on the floor, maybe if she would just look up, just once, she'd realize the whole pack keeps looking from her to me and back again. They know, and how could they not with not only our scent on each other, but the scent of our blood sifting through the air? I try not to think of our little rendezvous in the woods, but it keeps returning, messing with my concentration. I can hear her growls and feel her claws digging into my back all over again. Dammit this isn't good. I don't want a mate. Dammit Lee, I curse her silently.

"You ok buddy?" asks Marvin with a slight smirk and I suppress the urge to growl.

"Yeah I'm fine."

I hear the young wolf, Kaley speak up and at her suggestion of Lee leaving the pack I immediately feel a surge of irritation and anger go through me. Oh hell no, but before I can speak up, others in the pack do it for me. Before long they have decided she will stay. I'm surprised at the intense relief I feel, but I'm not going to examine that too closely. She's my friend, my packmate, end of story.

Martha takes Lee out of the room and still she hasn't looked up at me. I feel like crap realizing our lovemaking may have ruined the only female friendship

I've ever had, but before I can dwell on that for much longer, Gregory claps his hand on my shoulder causing me to turn back to my alpha.

"We need to talk," and although his voice seems calm for anyone near enough to hear, I can hear the underlying disapproval in his tone. I nod my head and follow him into the back office.

"Care to explain Shaw? I mean I know I told you to get Lee out of her because she was on the verge of a killing spree, but I didn't realize that meant you two would go off and return as mates."

"We're not mates," is all I think to say because even though we both have bite marks – We. Are. Not. Mates. "It was just a way for her to get under control," I say feeling uncomfortable and a tad claustrophobic…wasn't this office bigger before?

"You're not mates, but you just slept with and bit a fellow packmate? A packmate I might add, who has almost no control over her wolf and is going to snap any day now? A packmate who may have to be put down?"

"Put down?" I say outraged at the very idea of Lee being killed off like some sort of feral animal. "She's not feral," I find my voice rising and try to bring it back down, but Gregory has already stood up.

"Easy there Shaw. Be careful or I will put you in your place." I can see the anger burning in his eyes so I lower mine so as not to insult him further.

"She's not feral," I repeat again, more subdued this time.

I hear Gregory's weary sigh, and see him brush a hand over his tired-looking face, "I know she's not, but she could go that way. We have to find that werewitch and then get her to change as soon as possible. Every day she waits is another day something terrible could happen. If we have to force her to change, then that's what we have to do. Got it?"

I hate the idea of Lee being forced to become a wolf, but now that I know why she fears the shift, it all made more sense. I agreed with my alpha and yet I hated it all the same. "I think I can coax her into changing," I say, but Gregory threw me for a loop with his next statement.

"No Shaw. We were going to have you be her bodyguard until we can track down the witch, but after this whole mating/not-mating situation, I think it's best if you two stay apart for a while."

My wolf growls ferociously within me, outraged at being told to keep away from Lee, but this is what my alpha wants, so this is what I have to do. "I don't like it alpha, but I'll do as you say." Gregory nods his head as he walks around the desk to stand before me, "It'll be ok Shaw, we'll do our best by her, alright?"

"Alright," I repeat back, but there's a heaviness inside me I can't place. "Let's go get us a werewitch," I say with grim determination. Time to free Lee from her burden. My wolf and I desperately want to give her freedom. Freedom from her worries and fears. I want to show her that changing into her wolf won't hurt her or us. Our pack is strong enough to save her from a werewitch, and I'll do whatever it takes to keep her safe. A small part of my brain registers the possessiveness and protectiveness I feel for Lee, but my wolf is so wound up I ignore those questions, which I may later find myself regretting.

Chapter 8

Emmaline

LEE

Excited voices sound down the hall, "We've got it!" Peggy calls out, and I step from my bedroom where I've been waiting with Maggie. It feels like it is has been twelve hours since they left for the library, but really its only been about four. Maggie and I have been looking up werewitches on the internet and some of the information is totally ridiculous. Like completely laughable. Were some of those articles written by children? I don't know, most likely by crazy people anyway.

Maggie and I make our way to the kitchen because that's where we can hear Peggy chattering away. I'm feeling both anxious and apprehensive.

There are around ten wolves in the kitchen and they all stop to look at me as I enter the room. Shelby doesn't let the silence go on though as she waves me over to the stack of books Peggy and her have brought back with them.

"Now, everyone keep an open mind, ok?" We all nod begrudgingly as she flips open several books to pages they have marked with post-it notes. "We have no way of knowing what is true or false in these books, so Lee you need to tell us if the werewitch has mentioned any of these things or shown any kind of weakness or strength in a particular area, ok?"

"Ok," I nod my head as I start to feel determined...I feel determined to win. She is not going to run my life any longer.

I see dozens of images and none of them look like her. I describe her appearance again, letting them know the werewitch has never shifted form, either into an older human being or into a wolf. "She's only ever shown herself to be a young girl and she shows the personality of a young girl but a lifetime of wisdom resides in her eyes."

The room goes quiet and I realize I've stared off into space. I look to Martha, hoping she understands what I mean when I say the little werewitch is more grown up than a pre-teen girl should be, but still shows the traits of a child.

"Could be a trick," Maggie interjects into the discussion happening around the table. I think it over and shrug my shoulders, "Maybe, but I don't think so. My gut tells me she is a child, not an adult pretending to be a child."

"What kind of powers has she shown?" Martha asks.

"She can make herself invisible," I told them that before, but to have me tell them again seems to make them uneasy. "So she could be here right now and we wouldn't know it," Shelby states rather than asks.

"Correct."

Everyone looks around immediately, but we notice nothing strange. Not that we would if she was here.

"Also her power is blue. I noticed that when she used magic to pick me up and throw me against the shed."

"Okay so she has magic," Peggy seems to be thinking deeply about something.

"I think we do need Emmaline Martha," Shelby says after we've talked and discussed the information in the books for a few hours.

"I think you may be rig-" Martha is cutoff by the sound of voices murmuring by the front door. It becomes so quiet we could hear a pin drop in the kitchen as we all strain our ears to catch whatever the man are saying.

"Scared?" Maggie whispers in my ear, breaking the silence.

"A little. I never knew my real parents...not sure I really want to know them now." She gives my arm a squeeze to reassure me, "It's gonna be ok Lee. You're not alone." I smile back at her, "Thanks Maggie."

Before anything more can be said Bill and Marvin enter the kitchen. My heart is beating so fast, but from their slow pace and solemn faces I know the news isn't good. They share a look before Bill clears his throat, "Lee it isn't good news. There's no birth record for you. There's a few old newspaper articles about a baby being found outside of a hospital in northern Ohio. It basically asks if anyone knows any information to please call the number listed. There were no leads and you were adopted about a year later."

I absorb the information Bill has told me, or rather the lack of information. I take a deep breath in then exhale as I nod my head in acceptance. "Guess I'm not meant to know them."

"Don't give up," Martha says with a small frown, "Maybe Emmaline can help."

"How would Emmaline help with this?" I say skeptically.

Martha shrugs her shoulders nonplussed, "She's a witch Lee, who knows what all they are capable of."

"Ok, lets contact the witch. Let's ask this Emmaline." I hope this is a decision I won't regret.

~~~~~~~~~~~~~~~~~~~~~~~~~~~~~~~~~~~~~

WEREWITCH

So they're going to Emmaline are they? My eyes narrow with my hatred for that woman. They have no idea what they are getting themselves into, I think with a shake of my head. Part of me wants to warn Lee to stay away from the town witch, but I know she won't listen, she'll think I'm simply trying to keep her in the dark. No, this is a bullet I'm going to have to let her take and hopefully it will all be well in the end.

I use my magic to leave the pack's kitchen and arrive back at my cabin in mere moments.

"Not much longer, you don't have to be here much longer," I remind myself and I find comfort in that simple fact. "Thank you Nature," I whisper to the dark, empty cabin as a tear rolls down my smooth cheek and a relieved smile appears upon my lips.

~~~~~~~~~~~~~~~~~~~~~~~~~~~~~~~~~~~~~~~

LEE

I didn't have a very good night of sleep last night...too many thoughts of witches, werewitches, and a certain brown wolf kept going through my head. So I'm pretty darn exhausted and now I'm standing in front

of a small house with Gregory, Martha and Shelby on
the outskirts of Big Springs. It looks like a regular one-
story wooden frame house to me. It sure doesn't seem all
that "witchy," so this is going to be interesting.

"Ready?" Martha asks, looking me over.

"Ready as I'll ever be Martha," I reply
nervously.

"Don't worry Lee, she's nice," I know Gregory
is trying to reassure me and my inner wolf is definitely
calmed by my alpha's presence, but there is still a
nervousness within me. A nervousness for the unknown
and I hope this isn't a mistake.

Shelby knocks on the door and we all wait. I hear
the door unlock and see the doorknob turn, this is it,
gonna meet a witch. Breathe, just breathe.

A middle-aged woman appears in the open
doorway. She is not what I expected at all. She seems
kind and friendly as she smiles and greets the wolves

with me. Her hair is dark brown and curly and her eyes
are a beautiful emerald green. I notice they match the
gemstone she is wearing around her neck. She is shorter
than me by an inch or two and she is quite slim. Her
clothes are of good quality and complement her slight
frame. Emmaline is wearing a baggy dark purple
sweatshirt and pale blue jeans. It's not an outfit every
woman could pull off, but she looks good.

She seems nice enough, but I decide to tune into
my wolf to see if she picks up anything odd, she seems
overly-alert and I have to wonder why. My wolf has no
answers for me though, but I know Emmaline has her on
edge for some reason, so I keep that in mind as I watch
the witch called Emmaline.

"And who is this young pup?" she asks gently
and I break away from my thoughts as my eyes meet
hers.

"This is Lee," Gregory responds. Emmaline's
eyes look me up and down and she stares in my eyes for

a while, "You are quite a unique one aren't you?" I blink my eyes and look at my alphas and Shelby wondering what she is getting at.

"I am?" I ask with a little trepidation. I mean I know I'm unique because I was bitten and not born a werewolf, but she can't find that that interesting, right?

"Aren't you?" she says with a hint of humor in her eyes.

"Perhaps," is what I respond with because I'm not sure what to make of her yet.

"Come in, come in. Let's talk about your problem," she says as she opens the door allowing us to enter her home.

"How did you-" I begin to ask, but she gives me a smile that stops me from finishing my question. "I'm a witch dear and werewolves only show up on my doorstep if there's a problem they need solving." I see the others shift a little nervously, but Emmaline only laughs, "It's no problem dears, a witch gets used to such a life."

"Thank you again for seeing us on such short notice Emmaline, we appreciate it," Martha says calmly.

She leads us into the living room and we seat ourselves upon her large dark green couch. I look around the room as she announces she'll bring in some tea. There are all sorts of glass figurines lining the upper shelves she has placed along the walls. The shelves are a dark wood, perhaps mahogany and the end of each shelf has been carved into a fancy scroll of some sort. It's intricate and beautiful. My eyes wander over the figurines again, taking in the delicate patterns and the variations of color.

Where did she get these?

Did she paint them herself?

Did she collect them from her travels across the world?

Why do I think she has traveled?

Hmmm. My musings continue as I look from wall to wall. Some of the figurines are pretty and exotic, and others are a little grotesque and I'm unsure of what animal or person they are supposed to represent. A small chill runs down my spine as I notice a glass wolf...it is dying upon a rock, a sword stuck in its side. I shift my head to look away as I swallow down my revulsion, but I notice something, so I take another close look at the glass wolf. One of the rear paws is not a paw at all, but a human foot. I suck in a breath and lean back into the couch wondering who the heck is this woman and if I'm in a worse situation than I was before.

As I continue to take in all of her strange furnishings, my nose picks up some unique scents. I smell all sorts of herbs and spices permeating throughout the house. She must have quite a garden growing in her backyard to produce all these herbs I've never smelt before around the mountains of Montana.

As quickly as she disappeared, Emmaline returns carrying a tray with several pieces of white china upon it. No silver, how thoughtful. Yet I can smell silver in the house. I can't really blame her for having it though. Martha told me not to trust Emmaline a hundred percent and I reckon that logic works both ways, but now I feel more wary and I know its all due to that werewolf figurine.

As Emmaline sets down the tray we each grab a cup, it's the polite thing to do afterall and I already have one witch mad at me, I don't need to be on another's bad side.

"So, what do you want to know?" Again she surprises me with her knowledge of our situation and she must see the surprise on my face as she gives me another of her warm smiles, "Witch. Remember that dear, it'll save us some time."

We explain our situation to her – the abridged version. She interrupts to ask a few questions here and there, but overall she remains quiet with a thoughtful expression on her face as we tell her about our werewitch problem. After finishing our story we wait to hear what Emmaline thinks of the whole situation. I can hear the minutes tick by from a clock she has somewhere in the house, each tick is bringing me closer to lashing out. I thought I was a patient person, but I'm not sure anymore.

"I'll be honest with all of you, I don't know if my magic can beat her's." Finally Emmaline breaks the silence and I'm so relieved it takes me a moment to truly absorb what she said. I feel a sense of defeat come over me. "She's a werewitch and those creatures are quite rare, almost unheard of, and her magic is old, far older than mine." Our confusion must show so she elaborates some more, "The girl you describe and the information you know about her as a Viking child means she is practically ancient, and age usually means more powerful. I may be a witch with magic, but I live a human lifespan."

"So is there nothing we can do?" Martha asks, as the rest of us don't quite know what to say.

"I can look into my spells, maybe find a way to trap her or at least weaken her for you."

"Good, that'd be great," Shelby says with such confidence. I furrow my brow as our eyes meet and she says more quietly to me, "Lee it's a start. We don't plan on giving up and neither should you." I nod my head slowly in response, but I don't know if we can trust Emmaline.

"Well thanks Emmaline, we appreciate you hearing us out. Please let us know if you find anything that could be of use to us," my alpha states and we follow his lead by placing our tea cups back on the tray sitting on the glass coffee table.

"I will. I'm always happy to help…well unless it means I might die, but I hope you can understand that," she says with a soft laugh.

"We do Emmaline, thank you for time." Martha, she is so gracious because I certainly don't want to say "thank you" right now. I have a werewitch coming after me and so far I have no way to defeat her.

As we turn to head back to the front door the witch's next question has us all stopping, delaying our exit.

"Isn't there something else you wanted to ask?" Emmaline probes gently. I look quickly to Martha and Gregory, both nod their head for me to answer her. I turn back around to face those bewitching eyes she has.

"Yes...I, I would like to know where I come from. I was adopted in Ohio by a very kind couple, but I would now like to know who my birth parents were and the basics of my heritage."

"Hmm, normally I would say no, but considering you share witch's blood I'll help you."

"WHAT!?" I practically roar as Shelby and Martha both gasp in astonishment. I notice Gregory tense up, otherwise he remains calm. Oh to be an alpha.

Emmaline laughs, she laughs! "I'm not a witch, it can't be true!" I finish with a growl.

"Oh but you are my dear. I recognized it when I first saw you outside…witches have the power to recognize one another. I wonder if your blood is so watered down you can't feel it."

"I was raised by normal human parents," I say with some bite to my words.

"But they weren't your birth parents you said, so how can you doubt my word?" Emmaline isn't even fazed by the anger in my words, instead she seems to be enjoying herself. Witches, the bane of my existence I swear.

I grind my teeth together in frustration. I can't be a witch. It's not possible. It's not.

"Deny it all you want my dear, but you are one of us. I wonder which coven you come from?" I'm freaking out, Martha and Shelby don't know what to say, Gregory is looking at me with an unidentifiable look in his eyes and Emmaline's going on as if we're talking about the weather. What is happening?!

"It can't be true," I deny again, shaking my head furiously.

"One way to find out," Emmaline taunts gently and she knows when she says that what my answer will be. I can see in her eyes that she knows I'm going to say yes to whatever she's planning to do.

Chapter 9

Heritage Revealed

LEE

"Give me your hand," Emmaline orders me as we all stand in a circle around her kitchen table. Her kitchen looks normal, way less creepy than the figurines in her living room.

"Umm, no, how 'bout you explain what you're going to do to my hand first?"

"Lee," Gregory growls at me warningly, but I'm not backing down to Emmaline on this one. For all I know she may cut my whole hand off.

Emmaline merely waves Gregory off, "It's no big deal. I understand your apprehension Lee, but I'm not going to hurt you permanently. All I need is a little blood. I'm going to place that blood on this piece of paper," she unrolls what looks like an old piece of parchment and lays it flat on the table. The paper isn't blank, in fact it has several names written in bold black script. I scan the names and realize several sound semi-familiar from a history class I took so long ago. Wow this could actually be real.

Good.

Bishop.

Glover.

Osborne.

Proctor.

Hobbs.

Parker.

Hart.

Howe.

Martin.

Corey.

Nurse.

"These are the names of the original North American covens. That's right," she says as she looks at each one of us, "The original covens, as in Salem, Massachusetts."

"Holy shit," Gregory whispers under his breath and I let loose a small nervous laugh because seriously, is this really happening right now? This has got to be a sick joke.

"Not all the women were actual witches, and not all the ones who were set free were innocents. A horrible span of time in our history really - all those lives lost over something humans just cannot understand,"

Emmaline says with a weary sounding sigh. I can understand the sadness and relate to humans not understanding because we as werewolves have to lay low as well.

Suddenly Emmaline looks up with a hard expression on her face, "I know this information is pretty cool, but I do hope you won't go advertising this information."

"We can keep it a secret Emmaline," Martha grits out.

Emmaline nods her head once, "Good because we witches don't like to share all our secrets." After a short pause as we take in the unspoken threat, Emmaline continues, "So I will take some of your blood, put it on the paper and whichever name it travels to will be your heritage. It's not the same as tracking your parents, but still knowing some of your ancestors will be better than nothing. Won't it Lee?"

"Sure," I say, not feeling sure at all. I'm still hoping she's not right about me being a descendent of witches. Please let me not be part witch. I'm barely keeping it together as a new werewolf, how can I keep it together as a werewolf and a witch? Will that make me a werewitch? No, it can't be because I have no magic and I look nothing like the little werewitch I've seen.

"Give me your hand," Emmaline's repeated command forces me back to the present and away from my spiraling thoughts.

How did she convince me to do this? I scowl at myself as I reluctantly stretch my arm out in front of me. She takes my hand gently running her fingers along the inside of my palm, "Even the lines on your hand show your heritage. Do you truly not feel it?" she questions me, and I realize she's surprised I can't feel any power. Perhaps she is wrong then, perhaps I'm not a witch afterall.

"No, I feel nothing special other than the wolf inside me." Emmaline shakes her head at my response, pursuing her lips as she thinks about something.

Suddenly she brings out a dagger, a silver dagger, but as brain registers the threat she has already sliced a deep cut into my right palm. My breath leaves me in a hiss as the blade slices into my hand. "Damn, what the hell?"

Emmaline smirks as she moves my hand, "Sorry dear, I should have warned you it might sting more than a little. Silver is a weakness for you and will cause the wound to stay open longer – allowing us to use more blood."

"Fair enough," I say, but I'm not happy about it. My inner wolf was right, Emmaline can't quite be trusted. She may appear to be kind and gentle, and she seems quite helpful, but I think she's doing this for herself. She wants something too. I can't help but wonder how much I'll owe in the end.

Emmaline smiles as she draws my hand over the parchment and turns it face down. We watch as my blood drips down and splatters onto the faded paper. I stare intently as the falling drips form a solid circle of blood in the center of the paper. I hate to admit it, but some of this magic is as cool as it is creepy.

"That's enough."

I look up to see Emmaline nod at my bleeding hand, I close it into a fist and place it back my side. I can feel the wound slowly closing up and I know in just a few minutes my hand will look as if there was no cut at all.

Emmaline places her left hand about a foot above the paper and she begins to chant words in a language I have never heard before, but as her chanting continues they seem familiar to me. How strange.

We all gather closer and watch in awe as my blood slowly starts to move across the parchment. The blood weaves its own path amongst the names, drawing ever nearer to the name written in the upper left hand corner of the page. The blood stops on the only name left in that area, a powerful name, the name of *Proctor*. I thought I whispered it in my head, but I must have whispered it out loud as both of my alphas glanced my way.

My blood doesn't just stop on the name, but it gets sucked into the paper, disappearing altogether. Before my brain can fully comprehend that, my blood reappears through the name, turning every black letter blood red.

"Proctor," Emmaline says quietly, breaking the spell we've all been under.

"Proctor," she says again, more to herself than to us, "Yes, that would be right. A descendent of the powerful Proctor coven. That would make you the very distant granddaughter of John and Elizabeth Proctor. Elizabeth was tried and convicted of witchcraft in the late 1600s. John was the one to be executed for witchcraft though, and Elizabeth was spared as she was pregnant. She was later freed, and in doing so it kept her witch bloodline alive." She smiles before continuing, "Congratulations Lee, one of the mightiest witch bloodlines runs through your wolf veins. What a shame you never got to see your witch side grow." I don't know if Emmaline is being smug, condescending, or wistful. I feel so out of sorts it's hard to read her right now.

"Is that why she wants me because I'm a descendent of witches?" I can't believe I just said those words. I'm not sure my brain has fully registered that I'm a Proctor, or rather a descendent of Proctors, but I can't freak out right now. I'll do that later in the safety of the pack house.

"I think she must want you for a special reason, so I'd be wary of that reason."

"Is she going to try and kill me?" Emmaline looks at me thoughtfully before answering my question, "I don't know."

I nod my head, not willing to concede defeat, however I feel the start of despair enter my soul. My pack may want to save me from the werewitch, but don't they realize I want to save them from her too? It is time to make a sacrifice, and I know what mine will be.

"Proctor, that's amazing," Emmaline says yet again as she looks me over, "I'm a descendent of the Good family, a close friend of the Proctors. What are the odds." Emmaline has a strange look upon her face, one that puts my wolf on edge and my alpha picks up on it immediately.

"Let's go home Lee," Gregory commands and I cannot refuse. I nod towards Emmaline as the others make some polite small talk as we all wind our way back through the living room and toward the front door. I notice Shelby and Martha are standing closer to me than when we first entered the house. I imagine they can feel my distress and are trying to make sure I don't freak out. If I freak out now, I'm pretty sure Emmaline will kill us all if she can, so I am going to keep it together no matter what.

As I make my way to the door of the suv, Emmaline's voice carries over to us, "If you ever have any questions, I'm always around."

"Thanks Emmaline," I say politely, but I have no intention of calling her up at all. She may be a witch with magic, and she may or may not be able to help us take down a werewitch, but I'm not her latest toy to play with and my interest in my ancestors has not suddenly increased enough for me to side with a witch. I can use the internet as easily as the next person, so thanks, but no thanks.

Chapter 10

Evil Enters A Home

LEE

It felt like a normal day. It was supposed to be a
normal Saturday, but not everything happens as it
should.

The sun was shining, only a few fluffy white
clouds filled the blue of the sky. It felt like a perfect day,
but in my pack it wasn't a perfect day...far from it in
fact. Some of the higher-ranking wolves had decided
today would be a good day to take a bunch of us out on a
picnic. I know a picnic sounds ridiculous, but after my
confession a few nights ago and all the information that

has been thrown at us since - me being a descendent of witches and us possibly having no way to defeat the werewitch - well a picnic sounds real good right about now.

Martha said it would be a good way to help blow off some steam as the tension hanging around us had reached a new peak. We were all on edge and how could we not be? Here we are waiting, just waiting for the werewitch to make her move.

Obviously it doesn't help that half the pack still doubts me, and I honestly don't blame them. If someone had come up to me and said they could see something that nobody else could see…I would have doubted as well and thought that person was off their dang rocker. I'd like to say Annabelle's account of seeing the werewitch has helped add merit to my story, but the more distrustful wolves have it in their heads I may have manipulated the child. Me manipulate an alpha's child? Yeah right!

I let out a sigh as I finish wiping out the last of the coolers lined up along one side of the kitchen floor. I look at my handy work as Maggie whips open the freezer and starts pulling out bags of ice. I throw the dish cloth into the sink and help her pour the ice into the coolers.

At this point I kinda wish the witch would just make her move. I just want it to be over with. The pack doesn't know it, but I plan to give in the next time she appears. I'm going to let her win this one...consequences be damned.

My wolf nods in agreement – she's tired of being held down. She knows once we shift we may only live a few moments, but she's accepted it and I am thankful that we are of the same mind.

I smell a scent, a scent so familiar I close my eyes and pause in my ice dumping. My wolf perks up in excitement and I know, I know who is now outside the open front door. He's talking with the Beta about security measures for the picnic. I breathe in

It has been days since I last talked to Shaw, but it felt longer than that. I hadn't really seen him around either, except at a distance. My wolf wanted to talk to him, to be beside him, to feel his nearness. Her doe-eyed goofiness was getting to me. I would remind her Shaw was our friend and she would reply with one word, "*Mate*."

That's it.

I could argue with her until I'm blue in the face and still that was her only response. I guess one could say that my wolf and I had a bit of tension going on between us when it came to the mate topic. I was not going to agree with her about Shaw being our mate and she was just going to sulk about it. Of course I missed Shaw, he's my friend and I think he gets me in a way only one other wolf from my pack seems to, and that would be Maggie. Although to be fair Maggie is a strange one herself having her own secrets and problems to deal with.

"What's wrong?" Maggie's voice cuts through my thoughts and I snap back to the task at end, putting ice in the coolers and then filling them with food. I catch the mischievous look in her eyes, but I just shake my head as a handful of teenage wolves come in to help us.

"Nothing, I'm good." Maggie doesn't look like she believes me, but she leaves it alone.

I tried to shake off the sense of foreboding I had since I had woken up this morning, but it kept clinging to the edges of my brain. Something was going to happen today, something bad. Once again I tried to shake off the feeling as I helped pack up dozens of containers of food into several large coolers. This picnic wasn't going to be as simple as packing one cute little basket and heading off to the nearest tree, everything this pack does together is like industrial-sized I swear. Am I being sarcastic? Of course, but this is a lot of preparation for one lunch outing…into our own back woods!

Before long the coolers are full and we're now carrying them outside to load up the trucks. A lot of the cubs are playing tag in the front yard and a few of the mated females are reigning them in. I smile at both the playfulness and feistiness of the children. Too adorable.

Cars are being loaded up and the yard is emptying out, when suddenly the wind shifts, whipping my hair across my face. I turn to face the wind and hear a lonesome wolf howl high up on the mountain. My eyes search for any movement and I breathe deeply trying to catch the scent of the werewitch, but there is nothing.

"Is she here?" My alpha whispers behind me. I turn to face him, "No alpha, but that howl..."

"It's not one of ours," he says quietly. I notice several faces are looking through the car windows at us and I shift uncomfortably, "Could be Hal, but its odd for

him to be up there without having given me a call first."
His brow is furrowed in thought.

"But it could be him, right?" He nods, but we
both know what the other is thinking…it could be the
werewitch. Do we take the chance and send someone up
there after her? What if she is setting a trap? Do we wait
for her to come to us?

"Get in the car Lee," my alpha commands gently,
"She will come to us eventually and we will handle it."

"Yes alpha," I say with as much confidence as I
can muster. I want to believe we can handle what the
werewitch will throw at us, but she has power and
magic, and we do not.

I climb in one of the pack's suv's and buckle my
seatbelt. It is a very human thing to do as werewolves
heal so quickly, but it makes me feel safer. I feel a bit
guilty for not telling my alpha the plan I've come up
with, the plan to give in. I hope he and Martha can
forgive me when all is said and done.

A woodsy wild scent reaches me in the confines of the car. I've only been sitting here a few seconds at most, but I would know that scent anywhere. I breathe in sharply and grip the edge of the seat. I know my eyes have gone wolf, so I close them. I try to relax, but Shaw's scent has me wanting to wolf out right here in the car. I know he's two rows behind me – in the far back of the car and I can feel his gaze on the back of my head. No way am I turning around. I don't know what will happen if my eyes meet his like this, so I resist my wolf and stay perfectly still in my seat.

I don't want to chicken out and leave this car to dive safely into another. I know its not a long trip to the meadow, so I chant in my head that there are other people in the car, that I have enough problems without adding Shaw to the list,

The cars suddenly stop and my eyes pop open for the first time since getting in the car. Sweat has gathered on my brow from the internal struggle I've been having.

"We're here!" Shelby, the driver announces from the front & I unbuckle and dive out of the car so fast I probably look insane. I take a few deep breaths of the fresh air as I step towards the lead pickup truck to help with the coolers. I just need a task and to be far away from Shaw. I sense he's exited the car so I hurry to help unload the supplies.

For the rest of the afternoon I stay as far away from Shaw as possible, much to the irritation of my wolf. Man is she pissed! Luckily nothing happens and I make sure to keep a good twenty feet away from Shaw at all times. I also make sure to ride back to the pack house in a separate car because I'm not sure I could take that ride of temptation again.

SHAW

Lee and I haven't been allowed to be around each other ever since that night. I try not to think about it because if I do I can still hear her cries and feel her body pressed up against mine. I don't want a mate, but my wolf seems to have other ideas.

As soon as Lee entered the car, my eyes were locked onto her. I inhaled her scent, something fresh and earthy and my wolf lunged forward inside me hoping to get another bite of her shoulder. She never turned around once, but from the tension in her shoulders I could tell she felt the same.

She bolted as soon as the car door was open, making me feel both frustrated and relieved. Frustrated because my wolf wanted to claim her as my mate and yet relieved because I needed the space too. I didn't want to have a mate, and I knew she didn't either. It wasn't the right time and I was hoping we could keep our wolves under control until our mutual bite marks healed and faded. I was certain once the mate marks faded so would the desire to mate with each other. So I just needed to fight the urge for at least a couple weeks more and we'd be good. My inner wolf growled at the idea of letting Lee go, but that's the way it had to be.

LEE

I'm back inside the pack house. The coolers are empty and cleaned. The plastic food containers have been washed and dried. Kaley has opened the front door so we can move the coolers back outside into one of the sheds we use for storage.

I grab a cooler and start to walk down the hall when my eyes catch a flicker just as I leave the kitchen. I turn my head back around and the flicker has taken on a wispy form. A form I know so well. I see her appear completely in the corner of the room and my every hackle rises up.

"Get out," I say coldly, trying not to snarl. Out of my peripheral I see Kaley and Kelly freeze, but I pay them no heed as my eyes remain locked on the werewitch standing in the corner of the kitchen.

"No," she says with that now familiar smirk about her lips, and from the look in her eyes I know, I know today my time is up. Fine, let's get this shit started. I set down the cooler and let loose a small growl. I hear the gasps voiced around the room and I realize she has finally shown herself to my packmates. Well well, about time.

"Is that-" Kaley begins to ask, but I cut her off with a hard, "Yes."

Nobody moves as the werewitch and I continue to watch each other. I'm waiting for her next move, but she seems content on making me uncomfortable.

An outsider's voice reaches us from the still open front door, a voice that causes me to freeze at the utter look of unconcealed rage on the werewitch's face.

"Emmaline," she growls out and her eyes turn an even more luminescent blue, a cold cold blue, "What is she doing her?" she hisses at me.

"I don't know." Her sneer lets me know what she thinks of that. "I don't know, she shouldn't be here," I reiterate forcefully.

"Lee," Martha says as she comes into the kitchen followed closely by Emmaline, "Look who came, she says she has some information for us, to help us take down the werewitch."

I look at Emmaline and have to wonder why she didn't call first and how odd it is that she showed up just as the werewitch did.

"You!" Emmaline shrieks as she sees the little werewitch in the corner and balls of emerald fire immediately form in her hands. As I see the strange light in her emerald eyes my only wish is to save the werewitch behind me. When did I begin to feel loyal to her? I can't question that now, all I know is I can't let Emmaline hurt her. No matter what she's done, in my mind she is still just a child.

"Go away Emmaline," I order, yes I order the witch. She glares at me and I know for sure my gut instinct was right. Something is odd about that witch.

"Lee! She is here to help, move out of the way" Martha orders me. She is my female alpha, I have to obey…not this time I tell my wolf, not this time. My wolf and I fight the command with everything we have, locking my eyes on Martha I plead with her silently to release me from her order.

"Lee," she growls through her teeth as Emmaline steps forward, but still I refuse to step aside.

"Hmm, looks like you couldn't make her your new toy afterall sweet Emmaline," the werewitch cackles and I can feel her magic increase behind me. This is going to get ugly fast.

Gregory comes around the corner, taking everything in quickly, he also commands me to move, using so much of his alpha power my knees buckle. Sweat breaks out on my brow from the exertion of fighting the order.

Suddenly a calming hand touches my shoulder and instinctively I know it's the werewitch. "Lee, move.

I can take care of this myself. Move Lee." I cry out as I push my body sideways falling against the kitchen cupboards. I gasp for air as my weight settles on the floor and I can feel my alphas' rage at my disobedience.

"You don't understand," I gasp as I raise my eyes to theirs, "We don't need Emmaline. I'm going to shift. I'm going to let the wolf free so no one has to get hurt."

Before more can be said the witches start to let loose their power. Gregory shoves Martha from the kitchen and orders the others to stay back as blue and green sparks sing through the air.

I see Gregory dive low, landing beside me. He looks at me as the witches scream insults at each other and fireballs fly through the air scorching the surrounding walls, "I know you wish to make this sacrifice for us Lee and I'm so glad you wish to do this for your pack. You finally see yourself as one of us, but

I can't let you do this Lee. I protect each member of my pack, no matter what."

"What are saying?" I ask as more blue magic fills the kitchen.

"I'm saying I order you not to change. You will not shift Lee, do you understand me?"

I grit my teeth trying not to let the rage bubble out of me as his alpha power makes it impossible for me to refuse, "Yes Alpha."

"It's for your own good Lee," he says as he picks me up and runs from the kitchen.

Gregory immediately goes into action, ordering the young wolves out of the house and sending the cubs along with them. A few of the older wolves are sent along for their protection. We scatter looking for any kind of weapon, not knowing which witch will win the ongoing battle occurring in the kitchen.

About ten of us are gathered in the living room, including Shaw and Maggie. We hear several more shrieks, all coming from Emmaline before silence reigns. We strain our ears for any sound, but it is so quiet. A soft tap occurs and I realize it is the soft footfalls of a person coming nearer. That person comes around the corner...a little werewitch is what I see. And oddly I am relieved she is alive, why I don't know, especially when she has done so much wrong. But it doesn't change the fact that I am relieved, almost happy she is still alive.

"She's just a child," Liam was the first to speak and those were not the words I'd say to a werewitch whose done who knows what to Emmaline.

Her beautiful young face turns instantly harsh and cruel as she sneered, "I am not a child! I'm older than all of you combined!" She flung out her hand, sending small sparks of blue magic outward as she threw Liam across the room. His body landed with a dull thud. We were all crouched and ready to attack her, but a simple, "Nobody move, not yet," from the Alpha had us all remain in place, but low growls filled the room.

At our frustration a smile lights up her face making her look almost innocent, almost pure. Liam grumbles as he tries to stand, but the werewitch quickly puts a stop to that.

"Ah, ah, ah," she giggles while wagging a finger at Liam, "Stay down pup." Once again she lets loose her power and Liam slams down onto the ground.

"Stop it!" I hear the young voice of Annabelle cry.

In my head I'm screaming because Annabelle shouldn't be here, not now. Gregory sent all the cubs away from the house, including his own.

That werewitch knows Annabelle is a weakness for me and fear begins to creep through my veins as her eyes turn to face Little Belle. "What will you do for me if I stop?" she asks with an arch of her brow.

"Don't answer her Annabelle, get out of here," I say swiftly, in hopes of protecting the young girl.

"But," she begins to mumble, but immediately her parents command her to leave and she does with a sulky look on her face.

"Why are you being this way?" I demand trying to get the werewitch's attention focused once again on me. Luckily it works and those cool blue eyes hit me with laser focus.

"You went to Emmaline. Lee you should have known better, but I'm glad you have your answers. How does it feel knowing you are more like us? That you have the blood of witches in your veins?" Her questions seem so innocent and it almost feels like she cares…almost.

"Is that the only reason you want me?"

"Of course," she says with a hint of disdain, "I couldn't pick a regular werewolf for the task. You, you are special and I won't lose you, especially not to her," and her eyes begin to glow even brighter.

I decide to play her game and try to soothe her, "I'm not lost to you little werewitch. I'm right here. I never joined sides with Emmaline and I never will. It was you who told me to look at my heritage if I wanted answers. Where else was I going to get them if not from her?"

She seems to calm a little and I notice Liam is able to get to his knees, but a single glare from her has him staying there and not rising to his feet. Blood trickles from a cut above his left eye.

My wolf is angry and beyond upset, but she understands what I am trying to do and I think she's ready for the havoc that is about to occur.

"I concede that point," she replies with an air of maturity a child of her age shouldn't have. "Enough games Lee. I am tired of waiting." I gulp as I realize this is it, this is the showdown that has been building up for months now.

"Shift and let us be down with these games."

I try, I try so hard to shift it hurts, but nothing happens. My alpha has ordered me to stay in human form; I couldn't shift if my life depended on it, and it just might.

"Shift!" she orders again raising her voice. I feel her werewitch power begin to slide over my skin, but still I cannot shift.

"SHIFT!" she screams with the might of a true Viking in her voice shaking the house on its foundations. She is ready for battle and she has come fully prepared to get what she wants.

"I cannot," I cry out even as my shoulders bow to her awesome power and my legs collapse beneath me.

She glares at Gregory as she realizes I truly cannot change. "Stupid, alpha werewolf crap," she grinds through her teeth. With a wave of both her arms and a flash of her power she slams the rest of my pack against the walls of the room. Plaster dust rains down from the ceiling as the house absorbs such a heavy hit. I alone remain kneeled in the center of the room, exhausted from the efforts of trying to shift and being unable to.

"Where is my favorite pup?" she mutters quietly looking around. Her eyes fall onto Liam and I see the fear in his eyes as she wraps her blue magic around him and places his body beside mine.

"Let her shift alpha or watch another in your pack die!" she yells as she twists Liam's body, breaking both his legs. His cries fill the air and I can hear his mate's sobs.

"Please Alpha," I beg and I can see the tension fill his face even as his body remains immoveable against the wall. He doesn't want to let either of us die, but something has to give. "Me or Liam alpha, its one or the other. I have no mate," Shaw's growl echoes from where he is pinned near the picture window, but I ignore it, "I have no mate," I repeat again, "Free me. Please let me go."

I see the struggle going on within him, but he knows I am right. He must let me go or risk Liam's life. As Gregory delays a few moments more the werewitch breaks Liam's arms and more of his screams fill the air as his body convulses from the agony she is putting him through.

Finally my alpha has had enough, "You have my permission to shift Lee," his command washes over me again and I feel free of the strain I've been under for the last several minutes.

"Good alpha," the werewitch cajoles as she releases Liam. He remains motionless at my side. I reach for his shoulder in a sign of comfort and his soft whimper lets me know he still breathes.

"It's going to be alright Liam, you're going to be alright. Rest now." His eyes flutter briefly before remaining closed. I can only hope he's heard me and will lay still.

"Shift Lee or watch as I destroy your pack one by one." I look up and connect eyes with the little werewitch, so full of power, so determined. She won't back down and so I let the wolf come forth.

Chapter 11

Bang Bang, Everyone Dies

LEE

I feel the change begin, but since I've never shifted before I know this is going to hurt worse than any physical pain I have ever felt. I feel afraid, but my wolf tries to soothe me as my body begins to spasm and twitch. My eyes are now blue, my teeth and claws come forth, but that is only the beginning. I know the real pain will begin soon and I fear it, I actually fear the pain. Please let it be quick, oh please let it be quick.

SHAW

The werewitch has awesome power.

I knew it as soon as her magic rolled over my body the first time, and I continue to feel it, and I know my packmates feel the same as we remain pinned against the walls. If any of us had any doubt about her existence, it is completely gone now.

The werewitch is exactly how Lee described her. She has a smooth pretty youthful face framed by long white hair. I could see the Viking in her image and it did inspire awe. A being so old and yet she looks so young, so innocent. A perfect guise. Those eyes though, those icy blue eyes send chills down my spine and raise the hairs on the back of my neck. My wolf is agitated by the magic coming from her and I know the rest of pack feels the same. She is unnatural and she doesn't belong here in our home.

My eyes remain focused on Lee and Liam huddled in the center of the room. My wolf is pissed, not only because my friend is being tortured by someone who doesn't look old enough to go to middle school, but also because Lee stated she has no mate. When she denied me a rage like I had never known filtered through my every pore. I wanted to demand she take it back. Demand that she acknowledge me and my wolf and our claim upon her.

I knew the logic behind it and I know I am not her mate, not truly, but my wolf disagrees vehemently. It appears I cannot win on this matter.

I try again and again to fight the magic that has me pressed against the wall, but my body doesn't even move an inch. My fury increases at the helplessness of the situation. I won't let her hurt Lee, I won't. I have to help her, I have to.

I watch as Lee begins her first ever shift and I hurt as she hurts. I see the pain spiral through her limbs and I ache to hold her, to comfort her through the pain. Thudding footsteps have me shifting my eyes to the

entryway, it's young Kaley who busts through the door
with a shotgun in hand.

"Die bitch!" she screams as she cocks it and
takes aim at the werewitch who has spun around at
lightning speed to face her newest threat.

I see the werewitch flick her arms sending magic
towards Kaley, pushing her to the right. But the shot
rings out anyway, however it has found a new path. I
look to see where it hit and my yell breaks through the
sudden silence, "NO!" I reject what I see, but it doesn't
stop the blood that now spills from Lee's abdomen.

I struggle to break through the magic, but it
keeps me at bay, which pushes me over the edge. My
wolf starts to come through snarling and snapping to
protect its mate, yet still I remain under the werewitch's
spell, completely useless to aid Lee and barely half
shifted. I growl as frustration burns through me only
vaguely aware of the other wolves around me trying to
get free as well. I hate the werewitch, with every fiber of

my being. I hate the one who has done this to my Lee. I'm so far gone from my human side I don't try to reason the beast down, accepting in this moment that Lee is my mate and I need to get free to save her.

LEE

I am momentarily stunned – I've been attacked before but never shot. My eyes lock with Kaley's and I think her shocked expression matches mine, "Shit," we both say as I fall to the floor on my side. The rug feels a little scratchy against my cheek and the world seems to have turned a little hazy. I look down at my stomach and I can only see blood seeping through my shirt. My brain is on autopilot as I place my fur-covered hands against the wound to staunch the blood flow. So much blood. Blood, blood has me thinking of another time where there was so much blood...Jeannie. No, don't think of Jeannie, stay focused, stay here, stay alive.

"No!" cries out my little werewitch as she races closer to my side. My mind is numb taking in her concern and fear. She's worried about me? Does she not want me dead? She forces my hands away from stomach so she can assess the wound. I notice how her momentary distraction has caused her power to weaken and my packmates begin to slide down the walls.

"Lee shift, if you shift you won't die. Understand?" she asks as her small hand strokes my cheek. Her hand feels cool and comforting. I nod, still feeling numb.

She turns her attention back to Kaley, who is still holding the shotgun. "How dare you hurt what is mine!?" she screeches causing the glass to shatter from the windows. Glass shards are thrown about the room, slicing many of my packmates – yet I remain untouched.

Kaley dropped the gun and covered her ears, the only one of us lucky enough to do so. The werewitch's scream had my head feeling like it was going to explode. I try to focus my brain on shifting, but my head feels fuzzy.

Blue shards of magic leeched from the werewitch's hands before she launched them at Kaley. My sight came into clearer focus as I saw all that power blow through Kaley's young body like a dozen bullet holes. She fell to the floor instantly, dropping on her knees with her mouth open in horror. I saw the fear in her eyes and I smelled her blood as she folded, almost gracefully down onto the floor.

The werewitch has lost her focus and now the other wolves are free from the walls. They begin to edge forward, but my eyes remain on young Kaley. She turned her face to mine and we locked eyes. I saw the light begin to dim, "Kaley," I whispered amongst the howls and growls filling the room. She blinked once more and then she was gone.

"KALEY!!" I scream knowing she'll never wake. I feel not only my pain, but the pain of the pack as we absorb her loss. Tears fill my eyes at such a loss of young life. I turn my eyes back to the werewitch who seems to be calming down and an insidious rage burns through my veins, I roar as the change begins once again and my limbs begin to break and shift.

Let the wolf come forth I tell myself, let her do the damage that I cannot.

Chapter 12

And the Werewitch Always Wins

LEE

"Fuck you werebitch!" I scream at her as my blood begins to pool onto the floor. I can feel myself dying and I know what is coming next, unfortunately it isn't death. I hate the little werewitch for killing Kaley and I wish for her death.

The werewitch turns back to me with a surprised look on her face.

"She had to be punished," she says simply, "She hurt you, could have killed you and I can't let that happen Lee. You're too valuable."

"Go to hell!" I yell, but the words come out deep and garbled as my face is more beast than human.

"You're so ungrateful!" she cries in a childish manner more in congruence to her young looks.

Gregory launches himself at her, but with a simple wave of her hand she sends him flying out the broken front window, followed closely by Petroff and Maggie.

I sense Shaw and Martha drawing near to me and I feel safer as the werewitch looses more of her power. Shaw wraps his arm around me and pulls me back against the wall as objects begin to fly around the room. He tightens his grip as a lamp shatters against the T.V. and a vase smashes into the wall above our heads. Water and glass falls onto us, but that's the least of our problems now. The little werewitch is pissed and I have no intention of soothing her this time. The wolf inside is too furious and my human mind is too far gone to cage her back in.

Gregory launches himself through the broken window, half changed and a truly awesome sight to behold in his alpha fury. He has a dagger clutched in his paw and stabs the werewitch in the back, but its as if she can't feel it, sending him once again flying through the window, but this time she puts up a barrier.

"Shift," the child-like werewitch orders me and I can feel my wolf surfacing through my skin. I want to fight against the urge now, but I inherently know this is the only way to save my pack. There's too much blood loss, so my natural reaction is to shift into my dominant self, a.k.a. the wolf.

I feel the teeth in my mouth lengthen, the short nails on my fingers turn into sharp claws and hair covers all of my arms and chest.

"No," I hear Annabelle cry as she gazes in from the window, how is she back here again? "No" she cries louder as my body shifts more, but Maggie drags her out of sight.

I see Shaw turn to look at me there are cuts running all over his face, but his eyes are full of a burning intensity I'm not sure I understand. Is he surprised I'm finally letting the wolf free? Did my pack really think I'd let them die for me? Or is there something more in them I see? No, it can't be. I groan as more pain rocks my body.

"Lee it's going to be alright, just hang in there." Shaw's voice has thickened as his wolf is more present within him. He sounds so sure, so confident as pain rips along my spine causing me to spasm several times. "No Shaw, it's not going to be ok," I feel the words rip through my throat as my legs change. My body is so uncomfortable as I am not yet fully changed. I know I have to push myself more. I have to finish this.

My scream turns into growl as my nose lengthens into a snout, and I find Martha leaning over me – "Lee, just complete the change, we'll protect you." I barely hear her through the haze of pain and the sounds of snarling wolves and gunfire ringing through the room.

Who got another gun? I wonder absently before my body shudders once more – the change is now complete.

I'm panting hard as my wolf begins the healing process. I need to get away from the witch, that's what my brain is telling me and I try to get up, but I collapse back to the floor as blood still leaks from my wounded, fur-covered, body. I feel the pain, I feel death close by, and yet I feel the freedom, the rightness flow over me and through me as the wolf is now loose. We are so happy…I think as I look up to see the witch throw my packmates around the room like rag dolls and my moment of happiness fades.

Oh hell no, not my family!

I distantly hear someone roaring with anger, and it takes me a moment to realize it's me. Fury has finally gotten me up on my four legs, and I shake my head as my body sways, focusing on my target. A child, that's who I plan to kill…I sure have fallen far from my humanity.

I launch my body the short distance to her side. I clamp my jaws onto her small arm, inflicting as much pain as I can but she barely reacts. She looks down at me smiling, "Bad wolfy," she says before blue sparks fly from her fingertips and hurtle me through the air and into a wall. I crumple in a heap and there's just too much pain for me to stand up this time. I whimper as two strong arms come around me. I look up to see a very angry Shaw holding me close to his body.

"I'll protect you my mate," I hear him snarl as black dots scatter across my vision.

Did he just kiss my forehead? I don't know. He lays me down gently and throws his body at the werewitch. I whimper, fearing for his safety.

The werewitch finally seems to be struggling for control as more wolves attack. Her smile slips from her face and she stamps her foot in a childish show of her frustration. "I'll be back for you my Lee, you're halfway mine already. You can't escape it or change it. You were meant for me Lee, so says all the forces around you. I promise you this wolfy, you'll never escape me." And with one last spark of blue fire arching through the air she is gone.

The house seems so silent, so empty without her presence and her magic.

I try to breathe, but it hurts so bad, the pain keeps rocking through my body. I whimper again as blurry faces lean down over me and then my world goes black.

LEE

I wake up feeling something soft beneath me and I twitch my nose, realizing it is tucked up under a pillow. As sleep leaves me I realize I'm sleeping on a bed. I open my eyes and see I am still in my wolf form. I inhale to have the scent of someone familiar reach my nose and I'm startled to realize there is a warm body next to me in my bed. I lift my head, feeling only slight pain roll over me. I turn my head to confirm who is in my space and my eyes widen in surprise as I take in a half-naked Shaw. His face is relaxed in sleep and his hair is mussed. I smile inside at how relaxed his face is and how delectable his exposed muscles look. I shake my head to rid myself of that line of thinking. He's my friend, I remind myself.

Has he been there this whole time? I take a few moments absorbing his presence and feeling a shyness that surprises me.

I try to speak, but only non-sensical garble leaves my throat. IDIOT! I think to myself, of course I can't speak. I blow air through my nose in frustration. Before I think better of it I poke my nose under his chin. He startles awake, "What the?" he says and then sees me, "Oh its you, geez Lee," and he starts to chuckle causing me to give a small yip in response. I lick his face and he pulls away, using his arm to push me away, "Ugh, no gross, stop." I give another yip and then I get serious. I look around my room and then back at him, tilting my head to ask him for answers, but I can't, not in my wolf form anyway.

What happened?

That's the thought that goes through my head. That's the answer I need right now because I don't know what happened after I blacked out.

Is the werewitch dead?

Is everyone else alive and well?

What happened to Emmaline?

Oh my gosh, and poor Kaley.

I whimper and its like Shaw knows exactly what I'm thinking about as he reaches out his hand to softly stroke my head. "Yeah she died Lee, Kaley died." I lay my ears back as sadness takes hold of me. She was only trying to protect me, me the outsider and she lost her life for it. I don't think I'll ever forgive myself.

"We tried sweetheart, we thought we had the werewitch defeated, but she disappeared. We haven't picked up her trail and she hasn't shown herself around the house at all," Shaw's words hold no comfort for me. I feel more trapped than ever before. I hate this body, this life and yet I need to sacrifice more for my pack to be free of the werewitch.

With a sinking feeling I realize I've lost half the battle, I've changed into the wolf.

What was it the witch said? I'm halfway her's?

Does that mean when I turn back into my human self she owns me?

I lay my ears back and tip my head up, letting out a mournful howl. Why, why can't I escape her?

I hear pounding feet coming down the hall and my ears perk up at the unexpected noise. Half the pack crashes through the doorway, bursting into the room looking as if they are ready for battle. Maggie has a baseball bat raised above her head and Kelly is holding a cast iron frying pan, while Liam has a shotgun aimed right at me. Whoa.

Multiple eyes scan the entire space before registering that there is no threat in my room. They all take a collective breath before a smile starts to spread across their faces, I feel my lips pull into a smile too, well as much of a smile as a wolf can make. This moment of humor feels good, breaks up the tension we've all been feeling the last few weeks.

"Alright, alright there's no threat here, everyone out," Martha says and the group steps away, "You too Shaw," she adds with a smirk upon her face.

Hmm, not sure I like that.

Shaw gets up, stroking my head once more before grabbing his shirt off the floor and walking to the door. He spares me a brief backward glance before leaving me alone with our alpha female.

Martha waits a few seconds more until she's sure the pack has moved back into other areas of the house, allowing us a small amount of privacy. I can see the worry in her eyes and something inside me quakes. "Lee," she says gently as she moves into the room and seats herself gently on the bed, "We need to talk."

TO BE CONTINUED...

Made in the USA
Monee, IL
31 May 2021

69126423R00138